All That Glitters

by

Mickey J. Corrigan

All That Glitters

Contact Information: info@thewildrosepress.com

Cover Art by *Diana Carlile*

The Wild Rose Press, Inc.
PO Box 708
Adams Basin, NY 14410-0708

Visit us at www.thewildrosepress.com

Publishing History
First Edition, 2022
Trade Paperback ISBN 978-1-5092-4168-2
Digital ISBN 978-1-5092-4105-7
Published in the United States of America

"We should go into town, have drinks," Todd said, rubbing himself briskly with a striped towel that matched our chairs. "What say ye, Coco?" he asked, whipping the towel at me like he was in the boy's locker room at Yale.

I shrugged. "You know me, easy peasy."

"Darlings, no. We can't today. Remember? My sweet cousin is due any minute," Rose said.

It was the first I'd heard of it.

"Doyle is overdue," Todd said, then growled at his wife. She laughed way back in her throat, a hot purr.

I chugged my drink, glowering while the lovebirds kissed and petted. They looked like they adored one another but I knew better. He was cheating and she was bored to death.

Todd had just stretched out in the seat next to Rose, when a man in dress clothes appeared on the pool deck. He blinked in the razoring sunlight, then came toward us. His shoes were Italian leather loafers with a pretty buff. He sported gold cufflinks and a bulky Rolex. But I could see he was a working man, and not from wealth. Not like Rose and Todd.

He wasn't one of us.

Still, I sat up straight, sucked in my pouchy gut. Which was a bit bulgier than I liked from too much rich food and drink—and not nearly enough self-discipline.

Rose brightened immediately, and jumped out of her chair, her tanned and shapely arms extended. "Darling," she said.

"So we beat on, boats against the current, borne back ceaselessly into the past."
—F. Scott Fitzgerald, *The Great Gatsby*

"We never fall twice into the same abyss. But we always fall the same way... The abyss is bordered by tall mansions. And there stands History."
—Eric Vuillard, *Order of the Day*

Chapter One
In the Sunlight Zone

When I was young, my great Aunt Elda told me more than once to be sure to judge all books by their covers. Perhaps because she was an author of popular mystery novels, but more likely due to a snobbish approach to her world.

"I know the aphorism advises us not to judge, but superficial impressions speak volumes," she instructed me many times when I was a child growing up fast in her seaside mansion in Palm Beach, Florida.

Elda Leven was an immaculate person of exquisite tastes and immense expectations. She had spent her life in excited anticipation and grand disappointment. She never married, and I was her sole heir. Her hold on the purse strings, however, was as tight as her corset. A proper lady and a tough old bird, Elda was a powerful woman. I admired her almost as much as I loathed her. We stopped speaking when I began to take too long to finish my graduate studies. She had zero patience for my inability to write my thesis.

Elda had great influence on me. After the fatal car crash that took my parents when I was only nine, my father's aunt stepped up. She raised me as her own. We were constant companions as she groomed me to be a high society person, a well-mannered girl in a starched dress, shiny brown hair combed neatly, fake smile glued in place. A replica of herself, a chip off the elite block.

Fortunately and by choice, I do not resemble my great aunt in personality or desires. I am not a successful writer. I am an unknown poet and a scientist, explorer of the inner world and the natural world—truth not fiction, depth not superficiality. My poetry is dark and sad. Nobody wants to read what I write, but there it is—the sorry honest reality. I see myself as a reality instructor.

Elda's popular stories, in contrast, are clever imaginings set in a fantasy world that does not and will never exist. Life as a puzzling but amusing little mystery we might unfold rather neatly in a few hours or days. She would sip tepid tea with cream on a marble patio overlooking the turquoise ocean, dictating her formulaic stories. Not me. I hunched over the blank computer screen, exhibiting all of the telltale signs of downward mobility.

But that's the truth of it, isn't it? The reading public prefers to nurse on the tit of happy endings rather than open their eyes to the bleak reality of what we are doing with our lives.

Wasting them—and taking down the rest of the world around us.

Our differences aside, I have heeded Aunt Elda's advice on making instant assessments of others. Even now, as an autonomous adult, I do as she advised on that score, which makes me acutely judgmental. People make immediate impressions on me, impressions that stay with me, requiring striking amounts of further evidence for me to change my views.

This preamble is my way of introducing myself as

a biased sort of woman with a snooty upbringing and dark, revolutionary desires. But this story is not mine. It's not an autobiographical *novel* about my own youthful foibles. Nor is it a lush diatribe on the wanton destruction of the world's coral reefs, the focus of my graduate research and the subject of my thesis. No, this story belongs to my best friend from childhood, Rose McCrary.

You've heard of Rose, of course. Her short-lived high-profile modeling career. The dalliances with actors and athletes, billionaires and startup geniuses. You've seen her face on magazine covers and online, those liquid-gold eyes, the tawny skin, the blazing-white smile with such genuine warmth nobody can resist her. Now, just imagine being in her presence. In the presence of such purity and radiance. It's like sunbathing in early June on the Riviera. Imagine it, and you will understand why I have always adored basking in Rose's shimmery light.

We met as children, and she took a liking to me. I knew she was perfect the instant I saw her in the kiddie ballet class my great aunt signed me up for. Rose taught me the plié, and her smile was friendly in a sea of cold young faces. I had no trouble accepting her lack of depth because of the entrancing spell of her addictive sweetness and her flawless beauty.

Her beauty most of all.

Beauty is a door that's shut, a perfect illusion all viewers wish to maintain. You just fill in the picture with all the other positive personal attributes that should go with the person's stunning features, and you find this is enough. Do this with Rose and you will love her. As I do despite all that's happened.

The story I want to share with you begins and ends with Rose's cousin and his Palm Beach neighbor. And, of course, the great Getzstein.

Rose's favorite cousin moved to West Palm Beach in June of 2007. Doyle O'Henry had secured a rental directly across the Intracoastal Waterway from Rose, an off-island bungalow nestled in a grove of coconut palms and slash pines. A finance guy fresh off a Midwestern MBA, Doyle had landed a job at a small hedge fund on the island. Rose's husband Todd arranged the position. Todd had inherited so much family money he was able to arrange pretty much anything he wished. Anything his wife wished.

Over the years I'd heard plenty about Doyle O'Henry but had never met him. In the back of my mind was the idea our paths would someday cross. Once he moved into his bungalow, Doyle had a standing invitation to dinner at the McCrarys'. I wasn't waiting for him, but I wasn't not waiting either.

It was a sultry afternoon at the tail end of June the first time he came by. I had been staying with Rose for several weeks by then, and I'd finally settled down to business. I was there to avoid all distractions and write my thesis, so I had taken the summer away from teaching undergrad classes up north to isolate myself in the quiet perfection of the McCrarys' ivy-covered guest house.

In Boston, where I'd been living for years while dragging out my education, I'd been having a spot of trouble. I wasn't concentrating on fulfilling my graduate degree requirements, instead spending too much time with people whose book covers were torn and stained. I saw them and judged them disreputable, then found myself wildly attracted to them. I sat in windowless bars when the afternoon light had yet to dim, commiserating with the wrinkled ladies who thought life was a swift kick in the head. I judged the swaggering men in those places to be beneath me and unworthy of my attentions, then slept with them anyway. All to avoid the hard and deep work I knew I must do if I were to become an independent professional. Off the tit of the cranky old aunt, and all on my own.

The thought was both frightening and alluring. Hence, the internal and sometimes blatant struggle. Even after Elda cut me off to hasten my progress, I continued slacking and game playing with improbable men instead of acting the role of serious adult.

Alcohol in copious amounts was involved in my prolonged immaturity.

I was quite aware that I needed to escape from my downward cycle of bad habits and write. I was having a crisis of confidence, and it was taking all my time. To break out of the negative pattern, I had to focus on and finish my thesis. There's no honor in unused potential. No payoff either. Still, I kept waking up in the coffin of my own devise, my day-to-day life a futile scratching at the lid.

In short, I badly needed saving.

Because she was always there for me, always had been, Rose came to my rescue. She invited me to South Florida to work on my thesis. She would host me on the peaceful island of Palm Beach for as long as I needed, she said, and in the meantime, I could serve as an antidote to the profound boredom of new motherhood.

I arrived with a duffle bag of wrinkled clothes and

my laptop. I was pale and shaky but intent on staying clean and working diligently.

Rose was thrilled to see me. She looked even more beautiful a tiny bit plumper, which softened her, and her new-mother skin glowed. Penny was a bright little thing with pink cheeks and a bow mouth, but we did not spend much time with her. She had a bevy of nannies, uniformed Hispanic women who cooed over her and kept her dry and well-fed. It seemed I needed Rose more than the baby did.

I was ensconced in the coach house, the perfect writing retreat. The little cottage sat in a wooded corner of the McCrarys' three-acre lot. Under the sexy sway of royal palm trees and massive banyans that stretched their limbs for yards, the one-bedroom house had bay windows that peeked through the ivy to overlook the water.

Whenever I sat on the sofa with my computer in my lap, I could hear the gentle lap of waves against the dock. At night, I curled up in an Adirondack chair on the dock to watch the lights of West Palm blinkering until I was hypnotized enough to sleep.

I worked during the long hot days. I had a lot to say, and I was intent on presenting it in an unusual and striking style. My master's degree was in environmental studies, but instead of penning a long paper for peer-reviewed journals that would only be read by marine scientists, I'd decided to use poetics as my mode of communication. So my thesis was evolving into an Homeric ode to the former beauty and tragic loss of the world's coral reefs.

You see, my words had to be alive because coral is alive. Coral does not consist of blocks of petrified stone like I'd believed as a child but is made from hundreds of species of marine animals. The species that build coral reefs are known as hard corals. This is because they create a durable skeleton to protect their soft bodies which, when it is cast off, becomes reef material.

Other species of corals not involved in reef building are known as soft corals. These corals are flexible and look like underwater plants and trees. All of these coral species are beautiful, varied, and fascinating. The reefs built from coral grew very slowly, one tiny exoskeleton at a time, until they became massive features of our now rapidly degrading marine environment. Most reefs are five thousand to ten thousand years old, ancient undersea forests full of life.

Why this single-minded passion for coral? As a reality instructor, I wanted to raise awareness and instigate change, and there were two reasons for this. Growing up so near to the ocean, I'd spent many childhood hours in the warm water or walking the sand, collecting and admiring the chunks of what looked to me like rocky brain matter, and before they died, my parents were avid divers who loved the shallow waters of Florida and the reefs that live there.

Hence, my name—Coral Leven.

Maybe that's more than two reasons for my passion for coral. Suffice it to say, I am a passionate cheerleader for saving our coral reefs. Using the subtle but inciting power of poetry, I intended to stir up and bring to a boil the emotions of the blasé public, in order to sear them with the truth of what we are doing to our marine ecosystems. I intended to drive the blazing hot stake of reality into their tough little hearts.

But enough about coral and Coral. You want to

know about Rose. And her affair while I was a guest at her home in Palm Beach. And, of course, the true grit on the great Getzstein. Which means you must first be introduced to Doyle.

My immediate reaction to Doyle O'Henry was mildly but distinctively positive. He seemed bland. Safe. Upright and trustworthy and easy to control. He was good looking in a boy-next-door way, well bred, polite, smart but not wily. I wanted him at once with a migraine-like intensity, but I took my time. You have to with the decent ones. Or so I thought at the time.

Doyle was from the frigid hinterlands, a tiny town in North Dakota. His ancestors had grown wheat until the crops faltered, then they sold auto parts from junked cars they parked in their fallow fields. They sounded more foreign to me than Easter Islanders, and I was afraid to meet them.

But I did not get that far with Doyle. We broke up after only the shortest relationship. For that, I blame Rose. And Doyle's mysterious neighbor, Rose's lover, Gary Blass. But mostly I blame *him*. That monster among us, the monster inside all of us in Palm Beach—Jeffrey Getzstein.

Ah, the great Getzstein. He turned out to be my summer surprise, the ruination of everything, the extra dab of tarnish on the flaking gilt of Palm Beach. But I'm getting ahead of myself.

The day Doyle came to dinner at the McCrarys' was hot and sunny, of course, as it usually is in Florida in the summertime. Actually, it's mostly hot and sunny all year 'round. Since it was a Sunday, I'd quit pounding the keyboard early to join Rose for a happy hour lounge by the pool. The baby was upstairs sleeping, and Todd was swimming laps.

Rose and I lay side by side on her pink-and-white-striped chaise lounges, sipping our bloodies and watching Todd's muscular body slide through the popsicle-blue water. He has a tremendous build from a youth spent on the football field and another two decades working out with a personal trainer. Nearing forty, he looked much younger. A thick crop of dark hair. Tanned and jacked bod. Nice features and a dentisty smile. Todd was a dazzling man, a handsome creature, a lazy but beautiful animal.

Immense family wealth can do that for you.

When he pulled himself out of the pool, slick and shimmering, he splattered us with chlorinated water. Rose and I screeched good-naturedly, and he laughed, shaking himself like a big dog. The cool pool water felt good against my sizzling skin. I was wilting in the oppressive heat.

"We should go into town, have drinks," Todd said, rubbing himself briskly with a striped towel that matched our chairs. "What say ye, Coco?" he asked, whipping the towel at me like he was in the boy's locker room at Yale.

I shrugged. "You know me, easy peasy."

"Darlings, no," Rose said. "We can't today. Remember? My sweet cousin is due any minute."

It was the first I'd heard of it. I slipped on my beach cover, a man's white Oxford shirt, a leftover from a fleeing lover. I felt the need to hide my tanning oil-slicked torso. I wasn't in the mood to entertain strangers. My continued lack of productivity with the thesis had made me sour.

"Doyle is overdue," Todd said, then growled at his

wife. She laughed way back in her throat, a hot purr.

There was a bad taste in my mouth. I gulped my drink.

Fortunately, a maid appeared just then with a sterling silver tray of tall drinks. Two more icy bloodies and a crystal tumbler filled with Todd's preferred beverage—top-shelf Macallan. Only the best for the best, as he would often say.

I could use that line in my thesis. If I ever wrote more than the first page. Which I had written and rewritten over and over for the past two and a half years. That first page? I had probably written it seventeen thousand times.

I chugged my drink, glowering while the lovebirds kissed and petted. They looked like they adored one another, but I knew better. He was cheating, and she was bored to death.

Todd had just stretched out in the seat next to Rose, looking like a sated lion after a bloody feast, when a man in dress clothes appeared on the pool deck. He blinked in the razoring sunlight, then came toward us. His shoes were Italian leather loafers with a pretty buff. He sported gold cufflinks and a bulky Rolex. But I could see he was a working man and not from wealth. Not like Rose and Todd.

Still, I sat up straight and sucked in my pouchy gut. Which was a bit bulgier than I liked, from too much rich food and drink and not nearly enough self-discipline. I'd lacked any for so long I'd forgotten what it felt like to be proud of myself.

Rose brightened immediately and jumped out of her chair, her tanned and shapely arms extended. "Darling."

Todd opened his eyes, squinting in the cruel glare of the late afternoon sun. "My man Doyle," he said with a smirk. "Come to tell us islanders about life in the big dark hedges?"

Doyle blushed. He was pale, vastly freckled, attired in creased linen pants and a pressed cotton shirt in summer sky blue. He looked like a man on his way to a job interview for a sales position. He stiffened even more while Rose hugged him, perhaps because she was half naked in a neon-green thong, perhaps out of fear of being slimed with her coconut oil. Air kisses received, he appeared relieved when she replaced her bran-muffin butt cheeks on her lounge chair. Todd stood, and the two men shook hands, the cousin's slim fingers disappearing in the other man's giant paw.

I watched the three of them interact. Emphasis on *act*. Despite the glad-handing, the friendly banter and compliments, I could see that Doyle didn't approve of Todd, Rose was half in love with her country cousin, and Todd wanted him gone. Todd was a glutton for Rose's attention. He only tolerated me because I was like an old shoe that had been kept in the closet for decades, removed on occasion, and slipped on for old time's sake. Apparently, Doyle was something else entirely.

Rose stared up at him with abundant joy, her smiling face radiant, which made her cousin blush to a tomato hue. Todd dragged over a folding beach chair and placed it in the sun. He'd enjoy watching his wife's favorite cousin sweat.

Rose introduced us. "Doyle O'Henry, I want you to meet my oldest drinking buddy, Coral Leven."

I held up my glass and smiled, meeting his eyes,

which were a cool soft green. Like buffed jade or sea glass. My smile was weak, because my feelings were hurt. Alcoholic friend was not the persona I wished to convey to this man. Even though Doyle wasn't at all my type. He was a farm boy, clean and neat, good and straight. But I knew at once I would sleep with him. What I didn't know was how much I would care for him. And how quickly I would lose him.

"Tell us all about your job. Where do you go on all those weekday mornings in the wee hours?" Rose asked gaily.

Oh, she was a flirt. She riveted him with a greedy stare that said *whatever you tell me will surely fascinate.*

He began to loosen up, but I could tell it wasn't easy for him. "The fund is on Olive, an easy commute from my place. We get there early to check the overseas markets, get a head start on how the US market will fare that day. It's interesting. The fund managers are quite a bunch."

I could imagine. I'd probably slept with half of them.

Even though I was disinterested in learning the details, Rose kept at him. He went on and on to please her.

Finally, Rose asked, "Did you find a girl yet, Doyle? There are lots of pretty girls in Palm Beach."

By this time he was sweating. Furiously. The perspiration dripped off his pinkening nose. While chatting amiably, his eyes darted about, looking to see if he could ease his chair into a spot of shade.

I felt sorry for him so I stood, indicating my shaded chair was free. I removed my shirt and dropped it on the pool deck, then wandered over to the shallow end of the pool. I would get wet, then sit in Doyle's sunny seat to dry. I have auburn in my hair but not the redhead's fiery top and vulnerable skin like Doyle has. Still, I don't like too much sun, especially when dressed for a dinner party. He didn't deserve to be roasted on a spit just because Rose liked him.

Todd snored. I swam laps. Rose laughed and flirted, and Doyle relaxed in the shade. By the time I returned, he'd stopped sweating and seemed more content. He looked up at me and smiled. He had a nice smile, a good man's smile.

Rose squirmed in her seat, obviously thrilled to have her beloved cousin seated next to her. "Oh Doyle, I'm so glad you're here. We'll do so many fun things. The Norton, the masked ball, the winter galas. It'll be such fun!"

Doyle and I exchanged glances. Co-conspirators in the war on elitist shindigs? Our eyes locked, and I felt a tug in my loins, which did not surprise me. There was something delicious about this man, and I wanted a taste of it.

He had removed his shoes, revealing his long feet, white and clean. His shirt was unbuttoned, his broad chest hairless but nicely muscled. He worked out but not too much, just enough. When he spoke, his voice soothed. I could see he was good for Rose. He calmed her nervous energy. I wanted him to soothe me, too.

The maid called us to dinner with a jingling bell.

Todd sat up, his chin damp with drool. He stood, stretching his muscular limbs. "I arranged for us to eat an early dinner. I have an appointment downtown at eight."

An appointment? On a Sunday night? I didn't dare look at Rose. She'd complained to me for years about her husband's multiple infidelities. But since I'd moved into the guest house, he had not flaunted them. Perhaps a competitive spirit had arisen with Doyle's arrival, or maybe Todd thought we would be distracted and too stupid to figure it out.

I went back to my place to change and, I will admit, do some sprucing up. I wanted to look casual but sexy, natural but striking. It's a delicate balance, and working on myself is not something I often bother with. But I wanted this man to see me, to want me, to pursue me. Now that I look back on it, I think I may have been competing with Rose for her cousin's affection. But I had never competed with her before. Why would I? We both knew she would always, always win.

Rose was *that* girl. Every town has one. Head cheerleader, prom queen, girlfriend of the quarterback, every boy's secret or not-so-secret fantasy. I was lucky to be her friend, and believe me, I appreciated the role even as a kid. A stranger to wealth, an orphan living with a weird spinster aunt, I was tall and lanky, awkward and shy. I was so obviously from the wrong side of the tracks. I didn't dress right or speak right, not for Palm Beach. But Rose was my friend, and that let me in, if not to the innermost circle, at least into the shadows of that prized group.

When I arrived at the dinner table, the maid was pouring the wine.

"Here she is," Rose announced, smiling happily. "I love that color on you. Turquoise brings out your eyes."

She often said kind things like this to me, which made me love her all the more. Meanwhile, she was breathtakingly beautiful in a simple white smock embroidered with tiny colorful flowers. Todd wore a dress shirt, an Irish-green silk. He looked tanned and drunk.

He picked up the conversation where he'd left off. Rose rolled her eyes and gave me a smirky smile. She didn't say *boring boys,* but I read it in her expression.

"Have you read the latest UN report on climate? It's absurdist pulp. Scaremongering! I can't believe how much fake news the media puts out these days. I refuse to believe *they* believe the nonsense they promote to the gullible public. The news is all hogwash. We are completely restricted now in our viewing habits, our reading material. Nobody tells the truth anymore. And I, for one, resent that."

I'd heard his side many times before. There's no debating the massively entitled. So I waited to see what Doyle would say to this. Being from the Midwest and working in finance, he most likely leaned right. He might not think much of climate issues, which could be a red flag for a relationship with an opinionated activist like me.

Doyle held up his crystal wine glass. "I visited Borneo last year. They're thinking of relocating the capital city there. Moving Jakarta to higher ground. Can you imagine if we had to make that choice here, to move the financial district of Manhattan to a mountainside somewhere?" He sipped from the sparkling goblet, and the sunlight made his hair glow redder than the wine. "If we can have an impact on the situation, I think we'd better get to it. No matter whether you believe our problems are due to natural causes or from human activity, drastic climate events are a threat to all of us. Physically, environmentally, *and* economically."

"Exactly," Rose said with a tease in her smile. "Finally, a man at our dinner table who's not afraid to speak the truth."

"Now, Rosie," Todd began, but his phone buzzed, and he glanced at it where it sat by his fork on the white linen tablecloth. He snatched it up and, muttering *excuse me*, hurried out of the dining room.

Rose stared after him, her smile replaced by a mask of dread.

I kept eating my arugula and pine nut salad. Was Todd's call from a woman? Apparently Rose thought so, because she stood up and followed her husband out of the room. Moments later, her voice rose shrill and sharp.

I looked across the table at Doyle.

"Where do you stand on climate change, Coral?" he asked, his cow-fed face as warm and friendly as a pile of fresh hay.

"Shh." I wanted to hear what Rose and Todd were saying. I stood up and hurried over to the archway, listening carefully from there.

Doyle looked shocked by my behavior. "What the heck? What's going on?"

"You don't know?" I said after realizing I couldn't make out what was being discussed in a distant room. "Todd's got a woman stashed somewhere. Miami, I think."

Doyle sat back in his chair, his expression crushed. "Oh dear. Poor Rose. And with the new baby and all."

"Exactly," I said, returning to my seat. "If there's a time for cheating, it's during a pregnancy. But old

Todd, he couldn't even wait until the honeymoon was over to get himself a lady friend. The first in a very long line of dalliances."

Doyle shook his head, sad to the bone. "My poor little cousin. She loves him so."

Rose returned to her seat and poured herself a full glass of wine. Her face had lost its kittenish happiness, and her narrow shoulders drooped. The sun was still up, but the cast of late afternoon light was low enough that the room had shadows, corners dark enough to hide secrets.

Perhaps Doyle said what he did to cheer up his beloved cousin. Or maybe it was accidental, and he was ignorant of the backstory, which is what he claims. I don't know, but his timing was perfect.

"You girls should come over to my place, and we'll go to a Blass party."

Rose snapped to attention, her eyes wide and bright with interest. "Blass? You mean *Gary* Blass? Is he in town?" Her voice warbled, high pitched and full of excitement.

"Why, yes, he's in West Palm. He lives next door to me. In that pink-marble mansion. You know the one. And just about every weekend, he hosts a huge party. Live music or DJs, open bar, all kinds of people, crazy. I sometimes watch the throngs of partiers from my back patio. These bashes of his go on all night. I have yet to meet the man, but he left a note in my mailbox today, inviting me to come—and bring friends—on Friday night."

"Gary Blass, here in Palm Beach!" Rose cried out gleefully.

I dropped my wine glass. It did not break, but

expensive French Bordeaux spilled across the table. In the confusion that ensued with my stumbling attempts to clean up and my profuse apologies, the maid rushing about, all of us busy mopping at my mess, Todd returned to his seat at the head of the table.

"What'd I miss?" he asked, his tone the kind of swagger men get when they think they are worshipped by all women.

When Doyle started to speak, Rose cut him off. "Nothing, darling, but we're way ahead of you on the wine."

Todd took charge at once. "Soldad, leave the tablecloth. Bring us another bottle of the Bordeaux, the 1961 Lafite. Thank you."

And thus, the little dinner party resumed. We did *not*, however, resume discussion of the invitation to Gary Blass's, which I found delicious and intriguing, as well as supremely dangerous. I was liking this Doyle fellow more with each passing minute. He looked like a placid cornfield in the sun, but in reality, he had dirt under his fingernails and rough stones in his pockets. I wanted to get close to his milk-white bones to see what was hiding in there.

Chapter Two
In the Twilight Zone

I was alone in the blackness on the ragged edge of the universe. I'd had too much wine and not enough to eat, and my cluttered mind needed a good clearing out. So, after Doyle took his leave and the happy couple moved upstairs to continue their bickering, I took a lethargic stroll around the McCrarys' property. The night air was like a damp wool blanket, and a deep sense of gloom rapidly descended. I was restless despite the soothing calm of the natural world that hummed so prettily around me.

I stood out on the wavering dock, ignoring the McCrarys' fat white yacht to stare across the water that separated our island from the city of West Palm. Two different worlds, one glitzy and ostentatiously glam, the other up-and-coming overstated but with feet still planted in the dirt. Planted in Florida's weak dirt, which is largely sand, by the way, and apt to shift.

Little green lights flashed by, passing motorboats with shadowy drivers and quiet passengers. Tall skinny palm trees bowed and swayed in a steady breeze off the water. The hot air was almost too sweet, reeking of frangipani and night blooming jasmine. A white heron flew past, crying out for something lacking. A mate, a meal, a place to call home.

I selected a deck chair and sat for a bit, staring

across the lapping Intracoastal Waterway to where Rose's cousin lived. His small rental home was lit by a yellow lamp burning in a window, the buttery glow peeking through the clot of black trees. Life is looked at more successfully though a single window, or so it has been said.

Just to the north of Doyle's rental lay the vast expanse of spanking new, super-luxury excess that was, come to find out, the Blass estate. No lights were on, although on Friday and Saturday nights the house and yard were absolutely ablaze. Crowds of happy people shifted across the lawn, colorful knots of loud partiers. From the McCrarys' dock, you could hear the dense bass of raucous techno music, the deep and sonorous voices of DJs, and over it all the unmistakable sound of drunken laughter.

I closed my eyes, imagining Doyle O'Henry's sheltered life pre-West Palm. A skinny boy on a farm. A well-intentioned, studious kid, a young man accepted to a top university. Intense, hardworking, reliable. Serious, well-meaning, steady as a strong heart.

When I opened my eyes, the view across the way made it clear that Doyle lived in the looming shadow of Gary Blass. As did Rose. Because Gary Blass was Rose's long-lost lover, her god of all men. The one that got away. The love she really wanted but could not bear, except from a safe distance.

Now that distance had vanished, and Gary Blass was back in her orbit. He was living just there, right over the bridge, on the near edge of her sensory reaches.

After rustling about in all of my pockets, I found what I was looking for. I lit the wee joint and took a generous hit. Oh, Rose. New motherhood, a beautiful home, enough material wealth for a lifetime of lifetimes, and now what? Chaos and heartbreak. After all we had gone through together over the years, I knew my Rosie. I knew she always got what she wanted, and she still wanted Gary Blass. So I knew she would have him. She would draw him inexorably to her lovely self.

Closing my eyes again, I felt her magnetic pull, the nervous electric tug of her gorgeous physical being. The irresistible attraction that emanated from the master bed she shared with her bulky husband, a man of brute force. Todd had a cruel body and ugly sensibilities. I had never approved of him, and now, with his obvious display of extramarital adventures, I was rooting for her to leave him. Gary Blass could be just the impetus she needed to leave a difficult man.

But would life with Gary Blass be an improvement? I had no idea. I had not laid eyes on the man in five long years. We'd all changed during that time. The country had split down the middle with the haves on one side and the vast majority on the other. Which side was Gary on? It looked like he was on Rose's side, but what exactly did that mean?

I took another hit, brushing bits of ash from my thighs. When they were a couple back in Boston, Gary was broke and admittedly intimidated by Rose's family wealth. But now? From the looks of his rambling and well-kept estate, he'd made up for that lack with something exceptionally lucrative. An invention? A startup? Wildly successful financial investments?

Being with Gary Blass now would mean Rose would not want for much. Perhaps she would experience a tiny drop in status upon leaving the

McCrary circle, but other than that, her charmed life would continue to be charmed.

Or that is what I believed then, before I knew anything true, before the romance flared and flopped and all the chaos erupted.

I took one more draw on the magic weed. In the silent manse behind me, Rose slept beside her cold hard husband. Or more likely she lay awake in their canopied bed, her jackpot body stiff with betrayal and indecision, anger and lust. Sleepless due to the realization that her husband was no longer hiding his infidelities and her former lover was back within her grasp. After years of no communication and many tearful nights of grief, loss, and remorse, the tantalizing proximity of true love lay within reach once more. Big love waited for her just across the unquiet darkness of the lightly salted waterway.

High now, my mind swirled with old images like wispy dreams. I'd been there when Rose fell for Gary Blass, back when we were all students. Rose and I were Wellesley College girls, silly roommates with a penchant for hanging in dive bars. And Gary, handsome, funny, sweet Gary, bartended at an Allston dump we liked to frequent. He was putting himself through Suffolk Law, he told us. He was rough, redneck, but pretty, with light hair slicked back, a bit of shadow on a nice cleft chin. His smile was kind yet knowing. He was older than us. He'd lived. He was a man.

Rose and Gary, they came together like two hands in prayer. They spoke of marriage, children, and a life together in Boston. Her parents disapproved, but from a distance that, at the time, seemed adequate. Palm Beach was another world. Gary adored her, and Rose was mad for him.

Then it was the autumn of 2001. Tragedy, horror. Who can forget that time in our lives? Less than a year later, personal tragedy. I held her gently the night Gary left for Afghanistan, after she promised to wait for him. He had to go, he told her. Wanted to do it. He was that kind of man.

I stood beside her less than seven months later, still propping her up. I was dressed pathetically in an unflattering flounce of Crepe de Chine while she wept quietly beneath a gauzy white veil. The wedding was gaudy, gauche, exactly the way her parents wanted it. I drooped in the Palm Beach heat, my hands sweaty as I stood by my friend at the church altar.

I'd tried to talk her out of marrying the man her family had selected, the brash son of a diplomat, a bad boy with too much ego and an unhealthy amount of local status. I kept from her as much as possible the cheating scandals her fiancé liked to show off around town. Rose's heart was broken. She still loved Gary, but she was such a good girl then. Too much the good girl to defy the rules of elitist custom.

Impressive in his big man's tux, Todd whisked her around the polished wood dance floor at the reception held at the majestic Breakers Hotel. Heartbreakingly lovely in a modest but super-expensive designer gown, Rose managed to look the part of the happy bride. As they say, some dance to remember, some dance to forget. Knowing her as I did, watching this little act of hers brought tears to my eyes. And I'm not a crier. My emotions are usually kept tightly under my control. Part of my chill personality. The one I show to the world.

I got quite drunk that day, as did the resigned bride. We hugged each other for a few minutes at dusk, whispering platitudes. Then they left in a shower of rose petals, headed for the Port of Palm Beach in the back of a cream-colored Rolls. I was quite sure whose face she pictured in their luxury cabin late that night when her new husband mounted her. Her sadness filled my dreams for months while I finished out my undergrad degree and moved on to grad school.

The honeymooners spent two years bouncing around the best cities in Europe, another two lounging in the Turks and Caicos. When Rose announced she was expecting, the proud father purchased the largest estate on the market in Palm Beach. The shining couple returned to ensconce themselves on the brittle little island where we had all grown up.

Or had we?

A week after they moved in, I came by for coffee. I was in town visiting my aged aunt, trying to convince her to reinstate my monthly allowance. I had been barely scraping by in Boston on my graduate assistant's stipend. Still in school, I only had to complete my thesis to earn my master's in environmental studies. But I had nothing to say and I said it very, *very* slowly. My future career as an expert on coral was threatening to dissolve in a glass of bourbon. I feared I would flame out before I turned thirty.

Still beautiful and full of gaiety, Rose welcomed me to their new home with a big show of feigned enthusiasm. Her pregnancy was moving along nicely, and she was thrilled, she said, to be having a girl.

"A beautiful little fool," she told me, smiling through what I knew were not tears of happiness.

Yes, she was still so lovely and warm and thoroughly engaging as always. But my Rosie was not the same girl. She'd caught Todd on their honeymoon with a nineteen-year-old cruise stew, stunning the naïve bride into an immobilizing depression. He apologized, wept, made promises and vows, but his behavior continued in Paris, Nice, Rome, Venice, Barcelona, and Lisbon, most likely elsewhere. She told me that day over black coffee and fresh croissants that her heart had closed its doors, but she would not leave him. She was committed to seeing it through. She was a McCrary now.

I felt her newly acquired hardness, and it glistened in my eyes. Like a diamond formed from years of pressure on a soft lump of innocent coal.

****

The humid night enveloped me, and I kept on drifting. The weed had done its job—I felt light, full of scented air. The temperature had cooled a bit. Stars sprinkled like cheap glitter in the semi-dark sky. I'd seen my friend besotted, batshit with love and uncertainty, hollowed and bereft. Was I about to see her reunited with her beloved? Did he know his Rose was nearby, or was his choice to live in Palm Beach a miraculous coincidence? How could that be, with him next door to Rose's cousin and within view of where she lived?

And how had he made a vast fortune so quickly? From bartender and struggling law student to war veteran and then—what? Exactly where had his millions come from? Was he here in the crown jewel of Florida to impress Rose and win back her love? Or would he taunt her with his presence, his own happiness in a life quite rich without her?

I stood up, woozy from drink and smoke. My mind spun with questions, so many questions. Would Gary Blass reach out to his true love? Or would he choose to remain just out of reach?

No, I realized as I walk-stumbled inside the guest house. No, I was sure of it. They would reunite. In fact, I would *make* sure of it. Despite my coolly reserved demeanor, I am at heart a softy, a diehard romantic. I believe in love. Love above all else. Money is important. Material comfort is essential. But love, real love, is life itself. Without it, a woman fades, she ebbs away like the trickle of a spring shut off from its source. I didn't want to see my beautiful friend dry up and blow away.

I slept fitfully that night, my dreams saturated with vague images of desperation and want. In a bleak unknown place, I wandered alone down unlit streets crowded with dirty, grasping strangers. Poor homeless wags, women with black holes for eyes—suicide eyes. Battered women dragging their scrawny filthy children, babies beleaguered with rashes and scars. People with their unwashed hands out, their tired faces dripping, low, beggarly. Ragged men on beaten bikes rolling up and down the litter-strewn asphalt. People wrapped in silver-colored sheets, tinfoil blankets, locked in cages or on the loose, prowling trash bins for food. They appeared to be starving, many were raving.

In the dream I tried to ignore the abject suffering around me, to solider on and make my way to wherever it was I thought I was going. But I kept losing myself in a maze of waterlogged cardboard homes, crumpled sleeping bags on broken sidewalks, miles of steel cages lined up like honeycomb, endless as reflections in a hall of mirrors.

The vastness of their need, their immense lack, was sharp and painful, like a paring knife to my gut. I felt torn in two, pulled apart and opened to them. In the dream, I gave them everything I had—my purse and phone, my charge cards and bank account numbers, my inheritance that I had yet to receive from my tightfisted aunt. I gave and gave, ripped apart and rent, but I knew it was not enough. It would never be enough. Still bleeding and emptied out, I had become one of them, wandering the cold dark night in search of a way to survive.

I awoke to the sound of my own cries. I was yelling for aid. Whose aid, I didn't know. My entire body was covered in a light sheen of putrid sweat. I smelled rancid, like sour grapes. It was four a.m., too early for the beach walk I needed to shake off the existential dread of the dream.

I sat up, dizzy but wide awake and shaken. Screw the early hour, I would run to the beach, then return for a hot shower, strong coffee, and focused work. I needed to produce some pages, or I would hate myself even more than I had the day before.

Running shoes in place, I stepped outside, startling a pair of small owls standing together in the dewy grass. The speckled birds stared up at me with round yellow eyes like the ones on stuffed toys, unblinking eyes with huge black pupils. We connected, and I felt a strange and powerful emotion that lifted my heart. But they took off then, and I did not see them again for as long as I remained in Rose's guest cottage.

On those mornings when the words wouldn't

come, I jogged to the beach, then kicked along the white sand shoreline. Overcast days were best, reflecting my interior mood as the darkened ocean beside me gnashed, groaned, or held the quiet, brooding in and out with consistent, deeply mysterious sighs. Sometimes, the clear water appeared clouded over, the ocean queasy. On those days, the sound of the sea was a kind of keening. The waves seemed to be saying, *life on earth has never been easy, nor is it meant to be, but it does go on.*

You'd think I would be in the water much of the time, studying the coral. But I was not. I had completed the bulk of my research while an undergraduate, including a three-week trip to the Great Barrier Reef on a generous government grant. The Australian coral and the affiliated marine life were stunning. The widespread reef bleaching, however, was shocking and depressing.

Florida has the third largest reef in the world after Australia and the Belize Barrier Reef of the Mesoamerican Barrier Reef System. For this reason, I had come home numerous times to do my research underwater. The Florida Reef Tract is the only living barrier coral reef in the continental US, and it runs for hundreds of miles from north to south. This natural reef varies in height from a few feet to more than eighteen off the sand in what divers call "the land of the giants," where huge ledge formations hide sharks and big goliath groupers.

I'm not a fan of the deep water, but I love snorkeling, making coral reefs a good target for my underwater adventures. The Florida Keys provide the best snorkeling, but the inlets south of Palm Beach are also excellent places for shallow-water explorers like me. The coral living there delight with their startling colors—the orange elephant ear, the beefy red tree sponges, and ruby polyp octocorals.

In the crystal clear water, I've admired a variety of brilliantly hued tropical fish, including parrotfish in cornflower blue and teal, purple and gold damselfish, the long-nosed blue-spotted cornet fish, and the gold-rimmed butterfly fish with a striking black eye stripe. Sea turtles hang out by the reefs, and I once saw a little family of manatee, including a sweet calf. Also, to my dismay, I saw the occasional small shark, which fortunately always kept its distance.

Palm Beach County has installed numerous artificial reefs to support marine life and attract divers. The program began in 1985 with the public sinking of a Rolls Royce, a typical display of Palm Beach excess. Since then, the county has sunk dozens of old boats and barges, tons of limestone boulders and concrete. The Palm Beach County Reef Research Team keeps an eye on these artificial reefs and reports on the wide array of marine life they support.

It's a sad commentary on the human species when we feel we must dump luxury cars and ships into the ocean in order to improve the habitat there. All I've ever wanted was for the ocean to stay as vibrant and healthy as it once was, but that seems increasingly unlikely. Human behaviors are killing off the coral reefs and much of the marine life that has thrived on this planet for eons longer than we have.

No wonder the ocean keens.

That morning the ocean flitted in and out with soft whispers, coughing up dark-blue jellyfish, assorted shells, and the occasional chunk of polished sea glass. I picked up a rose-hued tidbit of salt-licked glass shaped like half a heart, stuffed it into a front pocket, then pulled it out later on my walk home. I rubbed the polished edges carefully like a magic lamp, wishing for more love for nature. Could we help heal the ocean and her coral reefs by changing our greedy, materialistic, narcissistic lifestyles? I thought so. But *would* we?

Such were my thoughts as I wandered along the empty streets of Palm Beach, past the towering stone mansions behind wrought-iron gates and the pastel boutiques selling trinkets that cost more than a year of groceries for a hungry family. Around me, the hibiscus opened their mouths to drink the morning dew. Big yellow faces, blood-red ones, bubblegum pink. Bougainvillea in magenta and cerise raged from sheltered doorways. The night air had released a heavenly scent from the flowering corn palms. Someone should bottle that aroma, I thought. It hypnotized you, made you believe the world was a sweet place.

When I reached my front door, I smelled freshly brewed coffee. Rose was inside waiting for me. She paced about with a steaming mug and a sickly smile on her tired face.

"About time," she gushed, coming up to hug me. "Oh, PU, you stink," she teased, holding her button nose.

Rose did not exercise and refused to sweat. She was naturally petite, her appetite birdlike. I had quite often finished her meals and, to stave off the fat, jogged or walked for miles nearly every day. I also drank more than she did. I ate and drank enough for the two of us, as she would sometimes point out with a teasing grin.

I moved past her toward the coffeemaker. "That's what you get for coming over before I've showered."

I sounded as grumpy as I felt. The planet was dying, and here she was, worried about her love life. I poured myself a cup, sipping critically to see if she'd made it strong enough. She had, thank god.

Rose stood on her tiptoes, stretching her arms over her head. They were long for her body, lithe, a dancer's arms. "Go shower. I'm taking you to lunch."

Lunch in Palm Beach is an all-afternoon affair. Drinks, or *cocktails* as the denizens like to call them. Endless meaningless chatter, salads so light they are fully digested before the coffee and whipped cream laden dessert trays arrive. Circulating with the wives of the super-rich is required. In fact, mingling is the sole reason for lunching in Palm Beach. It is certainly not for the food. No, dining out is for showing off your most glorious fortune and for feeling quite smug about it.

I let the hot coffee burn down my throat. "I have to work on my thesis today, Rose. That's why I'm here, remember? If I hang out with you every day, I'll keep procrastinating. I can't do that, it's just more self-defeat. More self-hatred."

"Oh, Coco," she cried, her wan smile fading. "I'm so sorry. I'm being selfish. Never mind, I'll leave you alone to do your thing. I *so* want you to be happy here."

She did, too. I believed her. But what would make me happy? Isolating for hours and days just to grind out more worthless and repetitive nothingness? Or spending quality time with my best friend, a beautiful woman whose true love had just magically reappeared in her life?

31

I looked at Rose. Her sadness exuded helplessness, her gentle heart pulsing visibly under a pale silk blouse.

Forcing a smile, I held up a hand, which was shaking slightly. I needed food. "Forget I said that. We have business to discuss. Boy business," I said, smirking for her sake.

Rose hugged me, ignoring my sweat. "I'll come back to get you at noon so we can go to town. Talk where we won't be overheard, make a plan."

I cocked an eyebrow, and she frowned, then nodded slowly. No, it was not safe to talk on her property. And yes, she wanted me to help her figure out a way she could see Gary Blass.

A plan was indeed what was needed. How to get the two long-lost lovers together in the kind of town where people with nothing but money and time thrived on one another's most private business. A town where men like Todd controlled the wealth and where women, typically much younger women, were their playthings, trophies, legacy bearers at best. The kind of town where babies were conceived for insurance purposes so that aging wives could be assured of getting something for time spent in service to wealth. A town I was within and without simultaneously, an observer unobserved. All the time I had lived in Palm Beach, I watched the rich folk flit around me like fish about a dying coral reef, enchanted and repelled simultaneously by the inexhaustible appetites of the world's most fortunate.

I stalked off to the shower, stripping off and dropping sweaty clothes along the way. If there were security cameras in the guest cottage as Rose seemed to be intimating, then I might as well put on a good show.

In the hot steam, I made a vow. I would do this,

assist my friend to reunite with a decent man who had once loved her. I would help create their love story like I was writing one of my great-aunt's cheesy novels, bringing the star-crossed lovers together for the kind of happy ending humans seem to crave. And rarely, if ever, get. After all, what is the true end of every life story? Death. For the rich and the poor, the lonely and the lovers. Only death waits for us all.

Although sometimes death is the least of our problems.

****

Dressed in summery frocks and reeking of coconut crème—me—and French perfume—her—we took the limo into town, leaving Penny with her nanny for the afternoon. Rose adored her white-blonde baby, a burbling cherub who made brief appearances in ruffled lace before being whisked off to the baby carriage or nursery rocker by a silent caretaker. Although Rose was loath to admit it, she was not an attentive mother. No, Rose spent her energy making sure attention was received, so she was ill adept at giving it. In fact, our long friendship was based on my ability to attend to her with the agreement that she would leave me alone when I requested it.

Which she did. Most of the time. Still, I had accomplished almost nothing that morning. I'd also done little when I was in my cramped studio apartment in Boston, facing the laptop screen uninterrupted and all alone. So when I was being honest with myself, I had to admit the difference in productivity was insignificant.

There was no one to blame but myself.

The sun was streaming gold, and the air-conditioned Mercedes was ice cold. Sitting quietly beside me in the comfort of the sleek leather backseat, Rose seemed small, vulnerable. I felt the old urge to protect her from herself, from her warped upbringing, the inescapable result of long years of brainwashing by the profoundly elite.

I reached for her, and for a moment, we clasped hands. Girlfriends. Besties.

Rose's driver spun down a side street to avoid the clog of downtown traffic. I glanced out the tinted windows at the city park, jacaranda and poinciana trees in full sensual bloom. A dozen homeless people wandered about, several lying on their backs on the dark-green benches. The town had discussed removing all of the benches on the island to discourage those without housing from camping out at bus stops and in public parks, but the city council had vetoed the idea.

Our driver stopped suddenly, braking hard enough that Rose and I lurched and slammed. He apologized, then swore softly. A bedraggled woman of indeterminate age stood in front of the car, looking in at us. She was pulling a beat-up shopping cart. In it were two naked babies.

My stomach roiled. The dream, the reality. This was so wrong. So much was wrong in today's world, but in Palm Beach, where carefully shaded eyes were blind to all but glitter and shine, it seemed criminal to be forced to observe the unnecessary suffering of the masses.

Rose didn't say anything, but her eyes widened and she clutched my hand. The Mercedes circled past them, moving slowly down the cobblestone street.

The driver dropped us at the eastern end of Worth Avenue, and we stood together on the whisked clean sidewalk, quiet for a moment. The image of those babies haunted, but we bucked up and discussed where we might dine. I was thinking how I could use a little hair of the dog, a bloody. Rose wanted to eat butter-glazed vegetables in an out-of-the-way place where none of her acquaintances would come upon us. Why then had we come to Worth Ave, where all the rich ladies of Palm Beach lunched after tennis lessons and personal training, manicures, and Botox treatments?

"We should have gone to CitiPlace," I said, "and tried not to get mugged. If you wear any bling to that mall, you can be sure someone will take it from you. But at least we'd know your uptown bitch friends wouldn't be there."

I was being facetious, but Rose nodded in agreement. "Oh well. Maybe they're all at Mar-a-Lago for the afternoon. There's a fundraiser luncheon today for erectile dysfunction." She held up one small hand, her fingers crossed.

With a twist of my own hand, I mocked with a less-than-erect middle finger. Rose laughed.

We strolled the Avenue, stopping to examine the most outrageous styles in the window displays. Ostrich feather jackets, clutches peppered with chunky gemstones, thousand dollar neon sneakers with four-inch ebony heels. Gold-dust chairs that looked like thrones. Fur-covered mattresses that looked like dead animals. Because they *were* dead animals. Gleaming cars parked along the curb ranged from vintage Duesenbergs to next year's sports cars. The number of red Ferraris was impossibly large.

Neither of us spoke much, both lost in our thoughts. If I had grown up anywhere else, I might have been impressed or horrified. Instead, I was bored, jaded, unmoved.

Suddenly, she grabbed my elbow. "Oh no, it's that awful Brit. You know, Jeffrey Getzstein's girlfriend. Not going to get stuck talking to that one. C'mon," Rose instructed, pulling at my arm.

We slipped down one of the bougainvillea-draped alleys to a winding line of small quaint shops. I pointed out an upscale bistro sure to have a decent bar. "Shall we?"

Rose agreed. "But we must sit inside, at their backmost table."

"Of course."

We ducked inside. I removed my sunglasses, and my eyes slowly adjusted. The bar was sunlit, but the dining area was dark, all ten tables empty.

Perfect.

A waiter in a crisp white apron approached us with a solemn expression. "Two for lunch?" he inquired, his voice discreet and mildly accented.

Rose told him our seating preference, and we followed him to the back of the café by the kitchen doors. We sat across from one another at a small round table with a white linen tablecloth and a brilliant red rose in a glass vase. I reached for the flower. It was fake. Plastic. Like everything in this town, I thought, trying to see inside the kitchen and failing.

No bloody for me today, I threw caution and thesis writing to the wind and ordered a bourbon, neat. Our waiter frowned at this, disapproving, so I said, "Make that a double."

Rose laughed.

"Such a naughty girl," she said after our server had

departed. She'd ordered iced coffee and a grilled veggie platter. Her new gadget, an exclusive and complicated smart phone, lay on the tablecloth by the silver. "Drinking your lunch again?"

I shrugged it off. "So, what's the plan? Surely you're not going to go to the party on Friday night with Todd in tow? We should arrange an accidental run-in. Or will you kayak across the waterway? Stalk him online until he figures out it's you? Oh, and why all the subterfuge at the guest cottage? Has Todd installed security cameras? Has he bugged all the rooms? Is he watching us right now on this phone?"

She laughed again, looking pleased with herself. Why, I had no idea. I was somewhat serious. Was her cheating husband really monitoring her? And, as a consequence, me? That was creepy. Strip shows were one thing, but I had shown off my sack talent in their guest house. I'd be mortified if Todd or his security staff had been spying on me.

The waiter brought our drinks, and I took a good swig. Ahh, nothing like sweet bourbon to start the afternoon downslide.

Rose emitted a soft gasp. A wild look had come into her eyes. "Oh my god, I think Getzstein's girlfriend followed us here. And she's with *him*."

I turned around to look out the front window, but the sunlight splattered there in a harsh spray and I couldn't see past it. I turned back to her. "Who? Getzstein?"

She didn't answer me but stared out the window, mesmerized.

Jeffrey Getzstein was the most talked about secret on the island of Palm Beach. Wealthy beyond all imagination, the man was handsome, single, successful, and brilliant. Being a billionaire earned you extra stripes in this town, and Getzstein was one many times over. Or so people said.

He owned a secluded mansion near the water and a private jet to whisk him off to his other properties in Paris and Manhattan, the largest ranch in New Mexico, and his own private island somewhere in the Virgins. He was also rumored to be a pederast who paid schoolgirls to massage his oddly shaped penis. Everyone in Palm Beach knew the sordid details about Getzstein, yet nobody did anything to stop him. No police were sent to his estate to order him to cease abusing little girls. He was, the men of Palm Beach said, eccentric. He was, their women said, a troubled person.

Yeah, and a dangerous pedophile. I for one wanted someone to do something about the sick perv ruining local girls' lives. But the man had friends in high places. Famous Hollywood legends and industry billionaires, British royals, American politicians, judges, and attorneys. And what if the rumors were true that Getzstein was connected to mobsters, that he threatened people, hushed them by saying he would have their families killed?

I smiled inwardly. Actually, if *I* stepped up, that might work in my favor, I thought. With no more Aunt Elda, I could lead a luxe life of drinking and debauching. I could donate big chunks of my inherited cash to nonprofits working to save the coral reefs while I lounged about Palm Beach with a tumbler of bourbon in one bejeweled hand.

Rose made a strange gurgling sound. The room

rang with her artificial laughter.

"What?" I asked.

I turned to look, squinting against the blaze of sunlight. And sure enough, there she was, standing at the bar. Getzstein's companion in teenybopper crime, the mysterious British heiress and reported procurer of her boyfriend's nubile nymphets. She was looking directly at us.

So was the tall man in a white suit leaning on the bar beside her.

But it wasn't Jeffrey. No, it was *him.*

Gary Blass.

Chapter Three
Mr. Nobody from Nowhere

Rose shook like a baby palm tree in a stiff ocean breeze. She cowered, too, hiding herself by leaning against the wall so that my body blocked the view from the bar. She stage whispered, "Go up there, Coco. Go up to the bar and order a drink. Say hello. Invite him to our table. Please?"

"Why would I do that? Let him come to you," I advised. "Let him come to us, his old friends."

Rose argued against that. "He won't take the initiative. Because I'm married. He would never do that. He knows it would be a *faux pas* to seek out a married woman in the town where she lives with her husband." She shook her head, disapproving.

But that was upper crust thinking. Gary was from northern Maine originally, land of heavy snow and tall, thick evergreens. Maybe you didn't have to follow the social niceties when your nearest neighbor was miles away. Maybe when you spotted your long-lost love across an empty room, you hurried over to be near her once more. Even if it was hopeless. Especially if it was hopeless.

Rolling my eyes at my trembling friend, I catered to her wishes, as always. With a dramatic sigh, I picked up my glass and walked slowly toward the bar. Gary and what's-her-name had their heads together, talking in hushed voices. They glanced up at me, their bland faces stripped of all emotion.

Gary looked different. Harder, more redneck, but cleaned up and polished over, rebranded in a way that did not suit him.

I gave them a look of contemptuous interest. "Gary," I said. "Long time."

When he smiled at me, I instantly remembered his incredible charisma. The way he was with everyone, male or female. How he gave off a welcoming tug of intimacy, providing a sense of full approval. He'd made a lot of tips as a bartender due to his ability to make his customers feel accepted, wholly and without judgment. I appreciated that about him since I was the opposite, critical and suspicious of everyone.

Gary's grin was contagious. His heartfelt humanity surged, engulfing me. I couldn't help it. I smiled in return as his love for mankind—and womankind— beamed into me, traveling though me, targeting my friend where she sat in our dark corner, food untouched, breath short, knees quivering under the table.

He straightened and held out a manicured hand. "Coral Leven."

I took his hand. It was cool and smooth like the rest of him.

Then he moved quickly, hugging me to his chest, which was wider, more muscled than when he left for Afghanistan. He'd been rangy then, hungry, striving. Now, he looked tended to, like a yard with a gardener. Care was taken, the natural beauty arranged just so. He smelled like leather and Cuban cigars. His breath had alcohol on it, like mine.

We air-kissed. "So," I said. "You're living here

41

now?"

"I am," he agreed, his smile white, stripped of all the old, individualistic, endearing imperfections. "I've got a little place on the Intracoastal."

The way he said it, I knew he knew that I knew exactly where he was living, but I played along for the sake of some antiquated propriety. Well, no, I would never do that. I actually played along for Rose's sake.

"Come say hello to another old friend," I suggested, taking his arm.

His suit was crisp, the pleats sharp enough to cut.

He resisted my gentle pull. "No, Coco, not now. I have a business meeting to complete."

He indicated Getzstein's mistress with a jerk of his handsome head. She was still leaning against the bar, her back to me now, drinking a cappuccino from a tiny porcelain cup.

I looked up at him, nodding curtly, conveying my disappointment and disapproval.

He touched my chin, lifting it so we looked directly into one another's eyes. His were a startling blue, the eyes of an Arctic wolf. "Please tell her I would like her to come to my place this weekend. I'm having a small party on Friday night. I'd like it if she could bring you along. And her husband. What's his name? Tom?"

"Todd," I corrected. We both knew he knew exactly what her husband's name was. "I'll give her the message. I'm sure she'd love to hear what you've been up to all these years."

As would I. And I was dying to know what he was up to now with Jeffrey Getzstein's sidekick. Why was he conducting a business meeting with the front woman for possibly the biggest viper in this writhing nest of poisonous snakes?

By *this,* I mean my hometown. Palm Beach.

They left before we did, but only because I forced Rose to stay put until they were gone. I refused to tell her what he'd said until we were alone again in the restaurant. The check sat by her elbow while I devoured her untouched vegetables and finished off my drink. Eventually, the waiter took her rich people's limitless credit card and disappeared behind the bar.

I mopped the butter from my lips and leaned in. "He's invited you to the party on Friday night. I think it's inadvisable, but I guess you'll go?"

She shook her head violently. "Absolutely not. No, no, no. I'm sure that would be a huge mistake. I must see him alone, talk to him without anyone seeing us, bothering us." Her voice crackled and popped.

I shrugged. "He doesn't think so. He invited me to come, too. And he said you could bring Todd."

She laughed then, a fake chirping sound. "Oh Coco, don't be ridiculous. Todd will never meet Gary. It cannot happen," she said, tiny tears forming in the corners of her eyes.

I reached for her cool little hand and patted it soothingly. "Okay, no problem. I'll go to the party with Doyle, and while we're there, I can talk to Gary. Set it up so you two can meet in private."

She squeezed my hand. "You are the very best," she said. "Whatever would I do without you?"

"Perhaps you'd eat your vegetables," I said, and she laughed. A rippling laugh, like a brook in the spring. That brought a smile to my face, and I felt my heart lift, knowing I could help the two estranged lovers reunite and spend time together. Perhaps something good would come of it.

On the way home, however, I started to worry. What was Gary Blass doing, getting involved with Getzstein's people? Their dirt rubbed off. Rose would have none of that. No upstanding woman would.

Beside me in the backseat of her limo, Rose had a dazed look on her face. As if she'd been the one to drink a double bourbon.

Back in the cottage, I had my thesis to avoid doing. So I napped, then went to work on the plan for Rose and Gary.

After a brief exchange of texts, Doyle O'Henry agreed to accompany me to his neighbor's upcoming party. But he insisted I meet him there, which I considered rude since he lived right next door. I would've preferred stopping to get him first so I could arrive properly escorted. Instead, I would have to dress not for a date but for a wild time. Most of my clothes were of the hang out and write in your torn tee and pajama bottoms variety, with little in the closet appropriate for dress up.

****

When Friday evening rolled out, I wriggled into a skintight beach dress with horizontal stripes in oceanic blue and green, white kicks, and a lot of dangly jewelry, mostly turquoise to bring out the blue in my eyes. When I was all ready to rock, I had a glass of chilled Chablis out on the dock while Rose instructed me carefully and annoyingly on what I was to say to Gary.

After the umpteenth rendition, I held up a hand. The hand without the wine glass in it. "Enough," I told her, rising from the deck chair.

Rose got up quickly and walked away, leaving her

nearly full wine glass behind. She trotted across the manicured lawn toward the pool deck, head down. She was subdued and hurt. But mainly my friend was worried I would blow it. She was relying on me, and I needed to reassure her I would do the job properly.

I slugged the wine in her glass, then chased after her. The sun had not yet set, and her halo of hair shone like a TV ad for a bowl of cornflakes. When I called out to her, she turned to face me. Her widened eyes warned me what not to say that close to the house.

Afraid of what could be picked up by security cameras, I hurried to catch up to her, then hugged her close, whispering in her pink shell ear. "Stop worrying. I'm going to give him your message exactly as you asked. I love you, and I want this for you almost as much as you do."

"I love you, too, Coco," she whispered.

I believed her, as she believed me. I am, after all, the only truly honest person Rose has ever known.

****

When Rose's limo crunched down the long pebbled drive that led to the front of the Blass property, I stared out the windshield in shock. I didn't recognize the place. I was used to the backside view with its wide sloping lawn, infinity pool, and pink-marble steps that tumbled down to hundreds of feet of waterfront, the Bali-style tiki bar surrounded by Italian tile decking, multiple statues of nymphets in scant clothing, and rows of chaise lounges in pastel prints. Your typical ostentatious nouveau riche backyard.

But from the street side, the house had a unique look. A squared-off cement block in a pale pink with a vast flat roof and thin vertical windows, it resembled an oversized cemetery vault. The house was surrounded by topiary in a variety of animal forms. Deer and flamingos, prowling panthers and flying raptors. Shiny new cars lined the circular driveway and spilled out onto the brilliant green grass, which stretched out like an endless plush carpet.

There were an awful lot of cars. All of West Palm must've been invited. All the excitement hunters together for one night of vacuous selfies and over-the-top displays of heedless excess.

The car door opened, and I slid out. Rose's driver reached for my hand, guiding me to my feet. "Might I suggest you text my cell for a ride home, ma'am? These parties, well...some opt to drive while intoxicated. I wouldn't want anything to happen to you on *my* watch."

He was still holding my hand when I realized I had never before looked the man in the face. I'd seen the back of his head often enough, observing his thick neck and wavy dark hair while he drove us to restaurants, nightclubs, and Worth Ave. I'd occasionally caught his smiling eyes in the rearview mirror, and we'd exchanged knowing glances. Now, I stood before him, his big hand in mine. An attractive Latino, powerfully built and with skin like Kahlua, a thick black mustache over full lips. Handsome, sexy, and very much my type.

Too bad about the wedding band. And the three kids under four stowed away in a dismal apartment in Royal Beach, which was rural and not at all royal and located many miles inland from any beaches. That's where the help lived until they could afford to move to a ramshackle rental cottage in crime-infested hotspots like Lake Worth.

Reluctantly, I pulled my hand away, my heart

pulsing in my throat. I managed to mutter, "Thank you so much. I'll keep that in mind."

I didn't dare ask his name. He was way too attractive. He would be much too dangerous, as would I after attending a party with an open bar, erotic dance music, and most likely the best in inhibition-blocking pharmaceuticals. I trusted myself less than I did this gorgeous married man, who was still watching me as I walked up the slick marble steps to the front door of the manse. I glanced back and he smiled.

Down girl, I told myself. You already set your sights on Doyle O'Henry, an appropriate partner. Keep them there, and you'll stay out of trouble.

Or so I believed at the time. But, as it would turn out, I might have been wiser to opt for a steamy affair with the McCrarys' Andy Garcia lookalike driver. My heart might have stayed in one piece. Rose might have kept her reputation. Everything might have been saved.

But I didn't know that then. I made what I thought was the wisest, even the moral choice, which goes to show you, not only should you always judge a book by its cover, you must also elect to read the ones that appeal to you most. Not the ones everyone else recommends. The books you think are so good for you may prove to be your downfall.

The front door was propped open so I walked right in. The wide foyer was a glaring white—white marble floor, bright white walls, a sparkly white ceiling forty feet up. Framed abstract oils splashed primary colors around the room, and a crystal chandelier the size of an airplane propeller directed visitors' eyes upward in shock. How in god's name did they get that thing up there?

A tuxedoed server passed by with a silver tray crammed with huge glasses that looked like finger bowls. Big shallow bowls of bubbling champagne. I grabbed one, thanking the girl, who giggled in response. She was Asian, her long hair in a thin braid down her slender back. She couldn't have been of legal age. Certainly not old enough to serve alcohol to out of control adults.

Had Gary borrowed her from Jeffrey Getzstein's stable of young mares? Was he, too, into the underage fillies?

After I chugalugged, a sick feeling settled in my gut. Not from the champagne, which was top notch. The queasiness came from a slew of unanswered questions. Who was this Gary Blass person my best friend was still in love with? What had he become over the past five years? And what was he doing in Palm Beach?

Chapter Four
The Inexhaustible Variety of Life

I set the empty goblet on a steel table cluttered with glasses and wandered through the first floor of the house. The high-ceilinged rooms were quiet because a majority of the party guests were outside with the DJ and the dance floor and the service bars. But I was not interested in joining the partying. Not yet.

As I meandered from room to room, each one more exclusive and tasteful and unlived in than the last, I searched for clues to Gary's new life. Who was he now and how had he managed to shed his dive bartender persona and launch himself into a *House Beautiful* life? I found no answers in his minimalist home. Living room, dining room, sitting rooms, offices, all were artfully decorated with the right amount of high-end furnishings and impressive modern art—sculptures, mobiles, paintings, delicate artifacts from around the globe. But there were no family photographs, no personal items. The house could have belonged to anyone. Or no one.

It struck me that Gary might be renting the place. Or borrowing it? But to what end?

Double oak doors to a room in the back corner of the house were closed. When I pulled on one, nothing happened. This one room appeared to be locked.

Suddenly, I felt embarrassed. If Gary caught me, he

49

would find my snooping strange, unforgiveable. Obviously, it was time to join the revelers in the approved areas of his property. Or someone's property.

I exited through sliding glass doors at the back of the house and stopped, staring out at the view. It unmoored me. It was as if I were looking in a funhouse mirror. My little guest house in the distance appeared forlorn, ivy-choked, dark, and untended. Todd and Rose's house loomed over it, a fat white hare squatting on a thick slice of green lawn. Security lights framed the view of where I was living as a picture postcard of extremes, and this unsettled me.

I needed a drink.

Gary's backyard was carefully lit. Overhead flashed multiple strings of tiny white Christmas lights while pastels swirled around the pool deck from the changing color wheel of an underwater lamp. The dance floor sparkled under a glitter ball of mysterious origins. The music was white rap, the crowd milling about mostly young. Very young. Much younger than I felt comfortable partying with. Across the pool deck, the dance floor, and the rolling lawn, kids in their teens and very early twenties sprawled and clotted, wandered and drank, laughed and leaned against statues, posing for selfies for distant friends.

I sauntered over to one of several bars set up around the pool, careful not to slip in the puddles of chlorinated water on the travertine deck. The lounge chairs held a bevy of trim bikini-clad girls, their overly generous boobs surgically perfected and peanut butter tans carefully sprayed on long lean limbs. Young men in brightly colored board shorts drank beer from bottles while chicks in tight neon tube tops sat on their laps or drifted from group to group.

A cluster of older gents in slacks and pressed shirts stood together by the bar, drinking liquor from cut glass, smoking cigars, and eyeing the girls. They weren't alone. Around the expansive yard were more men in their 40s, 50s, and older. But no mature women, present company excluded, could be seen.

If one considered me mature, which was debatable.

Getzstein's girlfriend came out of the pool house and stopped to chat with the cigar smokers. She was dressed in black leggings and a tight black tee. She looked like a dancer. At least she, too, was an adult.

While I stood there, scanning the crowd, I shivered. Something felt wrong. Very wrong.

A boost of liquid courage was required.

When it was my turn at the makeshift bar, I asked for bourbon, neat. The server was a cute surfer dude with long sun-bleached hair. He poured a generous glass and handed it to me with an easy smile.

"Are you a student?" I asked.

He shook his head. "Graduated last year. Took a gap year to determine what is next."

"Aren't you supposed to backpack around Europe and hang out in Amsterdam?" I asked with a friendly smile.

He shrugged. "I am from Finland. So I am exploring the life here."

Whoops. "You have almost no accent," I told him, embarrassed that I hadn't noticed.

"My mother is from New York," he said. "We spent a week in Palm Beach one winter when I was small. I always wanted to see what it would be like to live here."

I sipped my drink. "So, what do you think? Is this the kind of life you'd like for yourself?"

His casual smile faded. "I do not think so, no. I am here for fun but not too much. If you understand?"

"The materialism and excess on display in this town, you mean? Oh yes, I understand," I agreed. "It's way too much, right?"

His dark blue eyes narrowed. "Yes. And then there is so much poverty. Right next to the rich. And the way the men are, I do not like that much. We are not so in Finland."

Hmm. I was about to ask him what he meant exactly, but a clamor of girls underdressed in super-tiny jean shorts and midriff-exposing crop tops bounced up, looking for drinks. Or flirtation. Or both. The Finnish bartender got busy checking fake IDs and concocting the latest in trending cocktails.

I moved on, strolling over to the portable platform the kids were using as a dance floor. I stood watching the lively crowd, some getting down with partners, others making it work alone. The earsplitting music shifted jarringly from techno to pop to Kanye. I was bored. Where was Gary? And where the hell was Doyle?

When I turned too quickly, I bumped elbows with the man standing next to me. After apologizing for what was obviously my error, the man introduced himself as Felix from New York. He shook my hand. His grip was firm, confident. He was not handsome, but I could tell he was a player. Short, stocky, with smooth olive skin, he spoke quietly with a heavy European accent I wasn't able to place. His black hair was slicked back, his nails manicured, his tan suit an expensive-looking light wool.

Of indeterminate age, he was suave, his smile easy. This was a man who knew his way around a woman.

But he wasn't interested in me. That was obvious. From the first moment of our meeting, his dark eyes constantly roved, slipping across the shimmering yard, flitting from pretty teenager to teenager.

When I asked him what he did, silently guessing finance or fat inheritance from one of the legions of European aristocrats, he said real estate. I asked what kind, and he grinned. "The kind only very wealthy people are involved in. Not residential homes such as this, nothing so practical."

As if anyone could call Gary's immense manse *practical.*

When I laughed in surprise, he joined in. He was stirring the ice chips in his clear drink with one index finger. He stared at me for a moment, the smile playing on his lips. "And you?"

I launched into my well-practiced spiel about coral. His smile did not fade, but his eyes quickly skittered off. So I dropped the lecture and asked, "What kind of real estate do you sell?"

He sipped his drink. His smile curled in on itself. "Laundromats for oligarchs, mainly," he said and laughed. "I specialize in information. People want it. I have ways of obtaining it."

I believed him.

He told me his office was on the twenty-fourth floor of Trump Tower. "You've never heard of us," he said. "But you will eventually. We have big plans."

Unless he planned to save the coral reefs, I wasn't the least bit interested.

"So you're a friend of Gary's?" I asked, to see if

our host might be making—and hiding—money via Felix et al.

The man looked puzzled, then the leonine smile returned. "The host, you mean. No, I have not met the man. I am here in town staying with one of my clients. Jeffrey Getzstein."

Him again.

I excused myself after that and looked around for Doyle, who was still nowhere in sight. So I headed for the waterfront, where I pulled up an empty deck chair. The air was fragrant, redolent of tropical flowers that bloom only at night.

A small clot of underage girls stood at the near end of the dock, chatting. The sound traveled farther than they realized, making me privy to their conversation. Shameless, I sipped my bourbon and eavesdropped as they discussed the availability of party drugs and who had what.

Then one said, "I hear he deals at the local schools through Jeffrey's girls."

Jeffrey. Did she mean Jeffrey Getzstein?

A hippie chick in bare feet and a flowing multi-colored dress said, "I heard he killed a man. With his bare hands."

The third girl nodded. "Of course. He was in the war."

"No," said the hippie. "He killed a man who crossed him in business. I heard that from a, like, trustworthy source."

The first girl, a taut brunette in heavy makeup, argued the point. "That doesn't sound right. He stays under the radar. Right? He never comes to school himself, right? Or even hangs out with us here, at his own house. Not at Jeffrey's place either. I mean, Gary don't want trouble with *nobody*."

Gary? Were they talking about Gary Blass, our missing host?

I stood up and moved quickly to join them.

"Hi," I said.

Three pairs of clear, wide, teenage eyes stared up at me. These girls were under eighteen for sure.

"You guys know where Gary goes when he hosts his parties?" I asked. "I mean, is he here tonight?"

The hippie nodded. "Of course. I saw him out here earlier, but I think he went inside. To the library."

The other two giggled. What? Did the host read classic literature while the young people of Palm Beach drank up his liquor supply?

I must have looked confused, because the hippie girl took pity on me. "He's not into it, but he has his reasons. Everyone says he throws these parties because he wants his old girlfriend to show up. He really doesn't like parties like this himself."

"He's so romantic," the brunette gushed.

Her friends sighed, their unlined eyes shining with little girl fantasies and innocent desire.

I had more questions, but I was hesitant to ask them. About Jeffrey Getzstein and his girlfriend, about the young girls and the old rich men of Palm Beach. Still, I'd learned something about Gary's motivations. He was here to impress Rose. Maybe that's all this was.

I wasn't sure about their gossip regarding the drug dealing at schools or the killing of a man with his bare hands, but I doubted Gary would be involved with that kind of criminal activity. Were these just wild-eyed kiddie rumors about the generous, mysterious, and unknowable adult in their midst? Hopefully, that was all it was.

I thanked the girls and left the waterfront for the mansion. But before I could make my way through the inebriated throngs and up to the sliding glass doors, a hand grabbed my elbow. I spun around.

And there he was.

Doyle O'Henry. In white pants with soft pleats and a powder-pink dress shirt. His reddish beard looked burnished in the reflection of the Christmas lights.

"Hey," he said, his smile dazzling. "I've been looking for you everywhere."

Smiling, I said, "Same. When did you get here?"

"About two finger bowls ago. You?"

I laughed. "What's with all the teenyboppers?"

He shrugged. "Maybe Palm Beach adults don't want to attend a super loud pool party every week? I don't know. The crowd *is* kinda weird."

"Roger that." I was grinning. He was cute, and forthright. I liked him. "I have to tell you something. Come inside with me."

"Okay."

I led the way to the living room and a white leather love seat. When I sat down, I scooted over to make room for him.

Doyle stood over me, a goblet of champagne in each hand. "Reinforcements," he said. "Want one?"

I accepted his offer, sipping and wincing. Warm.

When he sat, our thighs grazed. Muscles bulged under the light linen. A runner for sure. I tried to concentrate, but it wasn't easy.

"Look," I said in a hushed voice. "Your cousin wants to meet with Gary, but she wants to be able to see

56

him alone. As soon as possible. Can you set it up?"

His face shifted from relaxed to uncomfortable. "Rose? And Blass? But why? Is this for business purposes? Like an investment proposal of Todd's or something?"

Doyle didn't know about Rose and Gary and their past relationship? I realized I would have to fill him in. I couldn't see any way around it. Besides, I told myself, he was as trustworthy as a man could be.

Later, I would recall thinking that, and I'd laugh at myself. What a dumb bunny I was. His was a book cover I totally misjudged.

"Rose wants to speak to Gary about something of a personal nature," I told him. Then I quickly summarized the backstory, providing a general outline of their affair when Rose and I were undergrads at Wellesley. I explained how crazy she was about Gary. "She's never been like that with Todd. Even before he was playing around. Marrying him was more of a business arrangement between their two families. With Gary it was true love. On both sides."

He sipped his champagne and listened as I rambled. He was a good listener. I felt the sweat form under my arms and drip down my ribs. The room was hot, and so was I. If I wanted Doyle to think of me in a more romantic way, which I did, I would have to change my approach. But not quite yet. First, he needed to agree to help me get access to Gary.

"I didn't know any of this," he said when I wrapped up my discourse with our recent run-in with Gary at the Worth Avenue restaurant. I did not say who he was with, however. I'd save that story for another day. "I'm in shock."

"Why?" Was a Gary-Rose dalliance so inconceivable?

He shrugged, his frown deepening. "I don't know. It just seems they're poorly suited. Gary Blass is an adventurer, a free spirit, a man of the world. Did you know he flies a seaplane? We're going out in it tomorrow morning. He just invited me to go with him."

I sat forward, so close I could smell his honeyed breath. "You saw him tonight? Where is he?"

He smiled. His green eyes shone like cola bottle sea glass. "I chatted with him in the library. He might still be there. It's an incredible room lined with hundreds of books and towering shelves that run right up to the ceiling, a dozen bookshelves just filled with books." He rose, setting his empty goblet on the artfully dented steel table next to the loveseat. "Come with me. We can go see."

He reached for my hand, and I let him lead me down the hall to the double oak doors of the library. He knocked twice, then pushed on the right side door and, to my surprise, it opened. Perhaps it hadn't even been locked before when I stood there feeling like an idiot.

I followed him inside.

The soft orange light cast from several antique desk lamps was dim, but the tall arched windows on the east wall welcomed the backyard glow. Outside, the men and girls came and went like giant colorful moths among the whisperings and the champagne and the brilliant stars above the twinkling water. The music was a soft, slow dance tune, a big band song from the 1920s.

Gary was perched on the edge of a long glass desk. He wore an old-fashioned smoking jacket in a plush rust color and held a tumbler filled with cracked ice and a clear liquid. He looked like an advertisement for liquor from the 1960s.

I smiled, and Gary winked at me, then said, "Doyle. She's so lovely. You're a lucky man."

My face felt hot suddenly, and I knew I was blushing. Doyle certainly was.

"Aren't I lucky, too, Gary?" I asked. "I get to see *you* again."

He sighed. "Ah yes, old times." He lifted his glass in a mocking salute, drank from it.

I realized he was drunk.

When he turned away to fix himself another drink, Scandinavian vodka from a cloudy white bottle, I crossed the room to stand before him. The Persian rug was so thick my shoes sank into the pile. I was still sweating and oddly nervous. He held a kind of power, here in his lonely kingdom full of strangers.

"How many books do you have on these shelves?" I asked, trying to capture his attention.

Without looking at me, he lit a thin brown cigar and inhaled deeply.

"I'd guess close to a thousand," Doyle said.

Gary scanned his collection. "At last count, over two thousand. Many are first editions. Some are signed." He glanced at me, and we locked eyes. "I have your aunt's books, Coral. All of them." My jaw dropped, and he laughed. "Don't act so surprised. I admire the hell out of writers."

"Thank you," was all I could manage. What else could I say to that?

Doyle came to stand beside me, sliding an arm around my shoulders. It felt nice there. Not romantic, just nice. "My cousin won't come to your parties. You can understand that."

Gary gave a curt nod and looked away. The blue smoke rose in the semi-darkness.

"So how can we help you with this, uh, situation?" Doyle said.

Gary sipped his drink. He didn't offer us one, which I appreciated. I'd had more than enough. "I would like to see Rose, and I'm hoping she'll agree to see me, too. But not here with nobody else around, that wouldn't look right. And not at her place. Obviously."

"She *has* agreed to see you, Gary," I said. "But where can the two of you meet?"

There was a moment of silence while we all considered the possibilities. A tucked away café in Boca? A small, obscure restaurant west of the interstate? Maybe a public park north of town, or a fisherman's bar in Jupiter?

Silence can be a black hole, sucking in the night and making it into nothing. Gary was drifting away. I could feel it.

Doyle reeled him in again. "What about my place? You both can come by in the afternoon while I'm at work. On a weekday. A workday."

That sounded smart. I nodded and smiled at Doyle.

Then we both watched Gary smoke and drink silently while staring blindly out the window. What was the man looking at? His past? We all harbor a desire for despair and ruination, for wretchedness. He seemed to be exuding this and with more gusto than anyone I'd ever met before, standing there with his stoic aloneness, his magnificent and wasteful elegance.

Finally, he finished his drink and set it down beside him. There wasn't much else on the desk. A clear glass paperweight, a gold pen, a short stack of hardcover books. "I still love her, you know. I've always loved her," he said in a low voice.

He walked out of the room, leaving through a door between two of the ceiling-high bookshelves.

Doyle and I stood there, kind of in shock.

"Well," he said after a moment.

"Yes, well," I replied.

We left the house.

Outside, the scene had shifted into something significant, profound. The meaning wasn't clear to me then, but I felt it as a stabbing pain in my heart.

We walked off the grounds, strolling arm in arm through the starlit night until we reached his softly lit bungalow. I didn't move to go up the slate walkway. I wasn't planning to go inside, and Doyle didn't invite me to. He offered to drive me home, and I accepted.

On the easy drive in his racy little sports car, down silent streets and across the Intracoastal bridge, we talked about our work. His love of rational things like numbers, mine of the mysterious beauty of coral and of poetry.

At the rotary, he pointed to Mar-a-Lago. "Do you know the history of that place?"

"I know Donald Trump the real estate tycoon owns it now. And that it sat empty for years." The wind caught my words, flinging them out into the starry night. I knew the history, of course. Everyone in Palm Beach did. I just wanted to hear this farm boy's rendition.

He was happy to show off his knowledge. As most men are. "Marjorie Meriwether Post, heir to General Foods, bought it as seventeen acres of scrub back in the

1920s. Around the time Palm Beach visitors first started snapping up properties for winter getaways. She named the property Mar-a-Lago, which is Spanish for sea-to-lake. Construction began in 1923 and kept some six hundred workers employed throughout the Depression."

"Wow," I said. "How big *is* that place?"

He grinned, his boyish face shining in the moonlight. "It's gross, actually. Something like fifty-eight bedrooms, more than thirty bathrooms with gold-plated fixtures, an eighteen hundred-square-foot living room with forty-two-foot ceilings. It's supposed to be a hundred and ten thousand square feet. She spent seven million on it, which would be like spending more than ninety million at today's prices."

I whistled. "Is Trump that rich? I thought he went bankrupt after his casinos in Atlantic City crashed and burned."

Doyle whistled a dirge, then laughed. "Get this. Post was a real philanthropist. Her plan was for Mar-a-Lago to be donated to the state of Florida and used as a center for advanced scholars. But state officials balked at the maintenance costs. So Post turned to Plan B— Mar-a-Lago could serve as the winter White House, becoming the property of the United States. After she died in 1973, the Post Foundation pursued the idea. But the federal government declined for the same reason the Floridians had. Too costly to maintain the place." He looked at me. "What a shame. That would've been so grand."

This was a story I hadn't heard before. "Yes, too bad. And now it will never happen."

Doyle turned down Rose's street, which was eerily silent in the darkness. "When Mar-a-Lago went on the market, it needed a lot of work. Nobody wanted it. The price declined and finally Trump bought it in 1985, at a deep discount. Only eight million dollars for all that waterfront acreage and the magnificent mansion with all of its elaborate furnishings. He turned it into a private residence for himself to use in the winter *and* a private hotel and club. The biggest snobs in Palm Beach belong to that club. Membership costs two hundred thousand dollars, and nightly rates are insanely steep. Still, the place is quite popular with the super-rich."

"Like Jeffrey Getzstein?" I asked.

Doyle didn't answer me. He eased up Rose's long drive while I instructed him on how to get from there to my cottage.

We sat in front of my place for a while, unwilling to part. So it was almost three a.m. when I finally made my way inside and flopped down on the unmade bed.

Doyle didn't kiss me goodbye, but we both knew what was forming between us. We shared with Gary Blass a haunting loneliness and with his partygoers the strange choice to waste our youth, to scorn the most poignant moments of our nights. To cast off, for unknown reasons, the most important minutes of our lives.

Chapter Five
In His Blue Garden

Despite my cynicism and general lack of interest in drunken bashes reeking of teenage angst, over that summer I attended additional parties at Gary Blass's estate. Doyle did, too, and after one of them I spent the night at his place next door. This was how we became lovers, finally.

The other parties were not much different from the first, loud and late with lots of alcohol- and drug-fueled youth. Each time I went whirling around that manicured backyard, tumbler of bourbon in hand, I took note of the ominous presence of older, wealthy-looking men. Some I recognized as well-known faces in town, elitists of the higher orders. There was even the occasional Palm Beach matron, typically flanked by her walkers. That is, gorgeous young gays who worked as underwear models and independent film actors. The people-watching was positively addictive, the celebrity sightings better than on Worth Avenue.

Getzstein's girlfriend made an appearance at every party I attended, chatting with guests, but I did not see him there. I rarely saw Gary, and only when I went looking for him. Typically, he was holed up in the library, and later on, before the parties came to an abrupt end, he was upstairs with Rose.

But I'm getting ahead of my story. After a quick

recount of some of the famous faces I spied at Gary's, I will return to my narrative.

One Friday I saw a former US president and the AG and two senators from a northeastern state. Another night, a Hollywood director, who has subsequently lost favor for his predatory sexual behaviors, and a famous actor rumored to be a rather violent letch. On another, a particularly hot evening where many of the guests ended up in the pool sans clothing, I noted the presence of a British royal, the head of a media conglomerate, and a Saudi thought to be one of the richest men in the world. At one time or another, I'd spotted a star race car driver and several world champion tennis players. Other athletes of note ranged from football greats to top golf pros. If I named names, you'd recognize them. Illustrious Palm Beach residents-in-attendance included bankers and hedge fund managers, as well as their attorneys, and the most infamous of the country's real estate developers. Russian nationals abounded, as did the Euro-trash *du jour*.

I guess celeb gawking was the draw for me that summer. That, and the opportunity to inhale free drinks with Doyle. He seemed as drawn to the wildness as I was, but in bed he was a meek lamb. On those semi-drunken weekend nights, I would devour him, and he would let me. But I will spare you the salient details.

The plan to reunite Gary and Rose had been delayed for the annual McCrary family summer vacation. Todd and Rose left town for a month, traveling in their yacht to the Mediterranean. Penny and I stayed home. I felt sorry for the baby, but the time was unusually productive for me. I ran to the beach every morning, then worked quite diligently most of the day.

After work, I had the grounds to myself for swimming and lounging unbothered. On the nights when I was not with Doyle, I sat under a shroud of fuzzy stars and thought about…well, not much.

One morning just before noon, Doyle called to ask if I would join him in town for lunch. I was fumbling for words that day, feeling like I had nothing lyrical to say about fringing reefs. So I agreed to meet him downtown and hung up with a big smile on my face. What kind of writer doesn't appreciate an excuse to stop working? None that I am aware of.

Standing before my closet in a sweaty tee shirt and running shorts, I scanned my clothes supply warily, wondering what I could put on that would be in keeping with Doyle's work attire. He wore pale linen suits and smooth Italian loafers, the uniform of the young banker in South Florida. I had nothing in my scanty dress collection that would properly complement the local business model. So I decided to borrow something from Rose's dressing room.

I walked right over to the house in my bare feet. I knew Rose wouldn't care if I lifted an outfit. We'd shared clothes for years when we were roommates. I was a head taller, my build fuller, more muscular than my petite friend's, but we could wear the same dress size because I preferred the bodice tight and the hem short. I wouldn't be able to fit into her slacks, but she might have a businesslike pencil skirt and silk blouse that would look appropriate if any of Doyle's colleagues happened by while we were lunching.

See, I cared about things like that with Doyle. Normally, I did my own thing and fuck 'em if they didn't like it. But Doyle was different. I thought he was a good person. I admired him. I trusted him. I wanted to help him, please him.

How silly a woman in love can be.

I let myself inside the McCrarys' through the servants' entrance and walked down the carpeted hall. I could hear Penny mewling upstairs, otherwise the house was silent. It felt quite gloomy with all the shades drawn and the air conditioning set too high. As if nobody lived there.

I called out a hello, but no one answered. So I went up the central staircase to the master bedroom. By that time, Penny had quieted. Faint, fairly tinny lullaby music floated down the hall from the nursery. I assumed the nanny was in there with the baby, and I went about quietly for I did not want to disturb them.

Tiptoeing into the vast room, I felt like a snoop. I wasn't trying to be sneaky, and I was well aware my visit might be on camera. Still, when I experienced that creepy sense of being watched, a prickle of fear crawled up my spine. As if it were wrong for me to be there. I had to force myself to continue on my quest.

Their bed was king-sized and canopied, harem style. Yet, there was still enough room in the master for a pale pink silk couch and two matching armchairs, along with a wall-sized television and a large wet bar. On another wall hung a life-size portrait of Rose and Todd on their wedding day, both looking charmed and quite smug about it. This brought back memories, and I shook my head. Poor Rose. Poor Todd, for that matter.

I crossed the thick pile to an adjoining room, which had been converted into a dressing room for Rose. Todd had his own room-sized closet down the hall next to the baby's room.

I had to feel in the blackness for the light switch, and when I flicked it on I jumped a little and squeaked out a tiny scream. Everything was tossed about helter-skelter, clothing in massive heaps on the floor and draped over shelves. I'd forgotten what a slob Rose was. We'd had small fights about that while living together. She had no regard for material things, or for order. The girl thrived on messes, on unnecessary chaos.

With a deep sigh, I picked through the piles until I found a black skirt and a floral top I thought might work. I'd give them both a quick ironing, and wear a pair of my flats. On my way out of the dressing room, I grabbed a jaunty cream-colored fedora with a fuchsia band that matched the flowers on the blouse. Rose didn't care for her clothes, obviously, but she had wonderful taste in them.

As I reached for the light switch overhead, a mahogany box caught my eye. It was sitting alone on a shelf. I recognized the Mexican hand-painted design from our college days. Before she dropped out to get married, Rose had kept all her favorite things in that box. Photos of boyfriends, love letters, corsages, ticket stubs, and newspaper clippings about herself from the style pages of Palm Beach publications.

I set the clothing on the bed and returned to the box. If there were cameras, I doubted there were any in the closet. So I stood there for a bit and pawed though my best friend's personal items.

I did this without feeling the slightest twinge of guilt.

****

Showered and primped to the max and dressed

appropriately in the freshly ironed outfit belonging to Rose, I took a cab to the bistro where I was to meet Doyle. When I stepped from the taxi, the noon sun brutalized me. The hat I'd borrowed helped shield my face, but I had to wander the bougainvillea-bedecked alleys for a bit to get to the address Doyle had given me, so I was perspiring profusely by the time I arrived at the restaurant.

In the umbrella-shaded courtyard, Doyle was waiting, ever the gentleman. His freckly face was pink from the heat, but it lit up even more when I approached.

"Wow," he said, "I've never seen you look so…" He stared.

"At a loss for words?" I asked with a grin. "Let me help. Devastating? Delicious? Luscious?"

He blushed a deep shade that matched my blouse and the band on my hat. "Um…all of those?"

I laughed and took his arm. "Please, can we sit inside where the air conditioning might prevent me from ruining my incredibleness?"

He guided us toward the doorway. "Of course. And I'd like you to meet one of my clients. Who just happens to be eating here today. He's my, well, my *biggest* client."

Doyle was warning me to behave. Grateful I hadn't worn cutoff jeans and a cropped sweatshirt, I winked. "I shall be the perfect Palm Beach matron. Nose high, voice well-modulated, pinky in the air."

He looked sheepish. "Thanks, Coral. It means my job. Apparently, they hired me specifically to keep this guy happy. Fortunately, he's been pleased so far with my efforts."

Doyle had talked in general terms about his position at the small firm on Olive Avenue. The company catered to exceedingly wealthy clients who needed advice on investments and the execution of banking chores at offshore locations. It all sounded questionable to me, as high finance usually does to those of us with low to no finances. But I was sure if Doyle worked there, then there was nothing shady about the business they conducted.

Silly me.

To please him, I stopped being flippant. In a more serious tone, I promised him I would be as chill as possible.

That was his cue. "I'm not sure that will suffice," he said, his head down.

My heart sank to my stomach, sending out a sharp pain that caused me to lose my breath. What did this man think of me? That I was a crazy woman, an immature bitch, a stupid slut? But then *he* winked, bringing my hand to his lips and kissing it.

Gotcha.

I laughed. And I loved him in that moment.

The bar area was lively, crowded, and loud with animated voices. The barroom itself was unusually bright due to floor-to-ceiling windows and a roof that was mostly glass. Tall ceramic planters with rangy palms were arranged about the room, providing privacy to the drinkers seated at small tables and in high-walled booths. Patrons wore suits and dresses in spring colors, and the flash of bling was nearly blinding. I stopped to stare at the beauty of the scene, enjoying the bounce of light off the gold, the blonde, the silk and leather.

"We can eat in the back room. It's less crowded

and a lot cooler," Doyle said. "But come meet Mr. Getzstein first."

Getzstein? What Getzstein? *The* Getzstein? The *great* Getzstein?

I dropped his arm and stood there, frozen in place. Jeffrey Getzstein was Doyle O'Henry's client? His most important client? The reason he'd been hired and moved from the land of the sheep to the lair of the wolves? The man he had to serve and, therefore, I needed to bow down to? A man with a reputation for a strong taste in teenage girls?

My face must have blanched, because Doyle noticed my reaction. "He's not what they say," he reassured me. "He's a good guy. You'll like him."

I doubted that. I wasn't in the habit of liking sexual predators. But I bucked up quickly, grimacing and quipping, "Show me to your leader."

Doyle smiled, obviously relieved. "Give me a minute to engage, then we're off. I promise."

He led me across the room to a booth in one corner that managed to be somewhat darker, more private than the rest. Getzstein sat there alone, hunched over his dinner plate. He appeared to be singularly focused on a bloody steak, silverware cocked in both hands. A fresh martini with two sunken olives sat by his elbow, which was bare as his shirt was short sleeved. Unlike the other gentlemen in the room, he was dressed in tennis whites, and he was very darkly tanned. His racquet sat across from him, propped on the facing bench. As if he were dining with his athletic gear. Or warning interlopers not to sit down.

I appreciated his abject lonerism in a town made up of herd mentality ass-kissers. But when you have billions of dollars to play with, you can pretty much do what you want in life. I had been led to believe Jeffrey Getzstein did just that.

"Hey, Mr. Getzstein. Here's the woman I was telling you about. The poet and environmentalist, Coral Leven. Coral, Jeffrey Getzstein."

I didn't reach out a hand as he was busy carving at that moment. And he was obviously not going to stop eating just to greet me properly. I forced a smile and a weak hello. I could've said, "I've heard so much about you," but that would have been tacky. Plus, I didn't want to get Doyle in any trouble. I'd promised.

Getzstein glanced up at me, and his eyes, an intense purplish blue, a weirdly attractive color, glazed over. "You've got a good man there, Miss Laverne. Doyle's one of the best," he said, forking a bolus of bloody meat into his mouth.

I agreed with that, and Doyle said, "See you this afternoon."

The man grunted, and we walked away.

"Thanks," Doyle said under his breath. "If you ever need me to return the favor with some marine scientist or a famous poet, I will be happy to step up."

I snickered. Fat chance of *that* happening. I was still light-years from completing the project that would determine my future career. If I even had one.

We passed by the bar, a long mahogany showcase manned by two handsome model-actors. As we stepped into the back room of the restaurant, I said, "You can tell my thesis advisor how hard I've been working this summer."

"I'd lie for you," Doyle offered, squeezing my upper arm gently. "I'd even die for you. How's that for the bottomless depth of my gratitude?"

He pulled me close and kissed the top of my head.

I couldn't fathom it. Why would he care so much that his client had given me a casual onceover? And how could a man as principled as Doyle O'Henry work closely with the person who had the most questionable reputation in town? A town *full* of men with questionable reputations?

An impossibly svelte hostess in a simple black shift and pearls seated us at a table for two. The menu was complicated, so I lost myself in the elaborate descriptions of fusion dishes while I attempted to stop my mind from running through all the questions I had for Doyle. If I wanted to keep seeing the man, maybe I would have to let this one go. And not snoop or pry.

But maybe not.

I set down my menu and leaned forward. "What the fuck?"

Doyle set his menu on top of mine. "I thought you'd say that, and you have every right to." I waited for him to explain, but all I got was a shrug. "Most people in town pay Jeffrey the subtle tribute of knowing nothing whatsoever about him."

I nodded, then cocked my head. As in, *go on...*

He stared at me, his green eyes like the ocean. Placid with the slightest hint of a potential for tempests. "In this world, there's only the pursued and the pursuing. You know this."

My turn to shrug. So what? I needed more from him than that.

Leaning in as close to me as he could get with a table between us, he whispered, "He offered me a financial deal one time. To invest my own personal money and make it grow exponentially. I said I had nothing to invest, which is true. I'm barely covering my costs, living in this town."

Cost of living is exorbitant in Palm Beach, so of course I believed him. I nodded my understanding, encouraging him to continue.

His low voice was hard to hear. "Just the other day he asked me to come to his house for one of his little parties. I said no. I explained our relationship was to remain strictly business as that would be best for safeguarding his fortune. He patted me on the back. As if that had been the correct answer." Doyle sat back and said in a normal voice, "For me, it was the only response."

This was what I had been waiting for. I smiled at him. "Can we get a drink?"

He said sure and soon we were enjoying ourselves the way we normally did.

I had a way with denial and was adept at deploying it whenever necessary.

Chapter Six
Interesting People

One morning in early August, when I arrived at my front door after an exceptionally steamy run, I smelled the aroma of coffee brewing. Rose was sitting on my sofa with a mug of coffee.

Even though it was *her* rattan sofa in the guest cottage where she was putting *me* up, I felt intruded upon. It took me a prolonged moment to remind myself about the reality of who owned what. In the meantime, I stood in the doorway kind of glaring at her until she jumped up to hug me.

"I'm *so* glad to be home," she gushed. "How've *you* been? How's the thesis coming along?"

I relaxed in her warm embrace, hugging her in return. I was good, but my writing had stalled out again. It really wasn't going anywhere. I had to face that fact. I hesitated to tell her, though, because I didn't want to look like a sleazy mooch, accepting months of her generous hospitality while I indulged myself in a love affair with her favorite cousin. Instead of producing the piece of poetic brilliance that would save the coral reefs and make my career.

I poured myself a mug of pleasingly strong coffee and followed her outside to the cluster of wrought-iron chairs on the back patio. A safe spot to talk freely. "Tell me about your travels," I said, kicking off my running shoes.

"Boring. I couldn't *wait* to get back here. I missed Penny desperately. I missed *you.* How's my sweet cousin? Are you two…" She batted her long eyelashes, wriggled her eyebrows up and down, and grinned.

What she really wanted to know was when she would be seeing Gary. So I said I adored her cousin, then got down to it. I told her the new plan Doyle and I had most recently concocted for the two estranged lovers.

"What if we have you over to Doyle's for tea? And Gary happens to come by? Then Doyle and I can make ourselves scarce so you two have a chance to get reacquainted."

Her smile was radiant. When Rose smiled with that much joy, she was almost beatific, saintly, as if haloed. "Perfect. Soon, I hope?" Her sparkling eyes searched mine. "This week?"

"Let me talk to Doyle. He can reach out to Gary." I smoothed her thin arm. Her tan had deepened, but she'd lost mass. As if she had failed to eat properly while they were away. "It's inevitable you'll see him again, Rosie, so don't fret. But what do you want from him this time around?"

She shrugged. "I have no idea. Right now, I just want to look at him. Close up." Her smile faded, and she spoke very softly. "Todd misbehaved so much on our trip. The drinking, the women. I could barely stand it. I'm tired of being so utterly disappointed in men."

I nodded. "We can hope that Gary Blass will not disappoint."

"And Doyle O'Henry," she said with a look I could not decipher. She stood up. "I'll let you get to your work. I'm going to spend the day with Penny. She's grown so much while we've been away. Babies are amazing that way."

And she'd missed it all, and for what? To be miserable in the company of a man who controlled her but did not respect her? What was the point in that?

A flock of white ibis had drifted down, gliding into place around us on the trim lawn. Ignoring the humans, they'd been stalking the grass, digging for insects with their curved salmon-colored bills. As we headed back inside, however, they lifted off as one, perhaps leaving us for greener, buggier pastures.

I walked her through the cottage to the front door. "We'll make this happen soon," I promised my dear friend.

She hugged me tight. Like I was doing her a huge favor.

At the time, I believed I was doing exactly that.

****

Showered and caffeinated, I sat cross-legged on the sofa, laptop in position. I would write today. I would write beautifully, truthfully and deeply.

My cell buzzed. Doyle. I answered.

"Gary just called me. He said the McCrarys arrived home late last night. He's been watching the house, I guess. Anyway, he wants to see her day after tomorrow. He says he doesn't want to put me to any trouble, but he can't invite her to his place, so they couldn't be alone there. He's agreed to our idea. And, so…well, looks like *our* plan is on."

I laughed softly. "Rose was just here. She's up for it, too."

He grunted. "Okay, then tell her four o'clock

Saturday. And not to bring Todd."

"Todd? Who's Todd?" I joked. Then I said, "He plays tennis and hangs out at his club on Saturday afternoons, supposedly. Or maybe he's with a mistress. Either way, Saturday should work."

We chatted for a moment, then hung up. I went back to my laptop and, I hoped, a few hours of productivity on the thesis. My heart was in it, and occasionally my head followed. I knew what I wished to say. It was just so difficult to say it lyrically. What I wanted the world to understand is our intense cohabitation. How we depend on one another for life itself. Coral is part of that symbiosis. If only we would all recognize that.

Coral needed protecting. My thesis needed writing. I was determined to do my part.

****

On Saturday morning, Doyle called to tell me Gary had hired a man to mow the grass. Doyle's grass at his rented bungalow, which the landlord had been neglecting. A florist's van had arrived at eight a.m. with a delivery and dozens of bouquets in delicate crystal vases.

Doyle sounded flummoxed. He needed help with the tea things.

I was looking for an excuse to avoid sitting in front of the blank screen, so I immediately volunteered to run to the local bakery for supplies, then come straight over.

Doyle sighed with relief. "Thank you. You're an angel of mercy."

First time anyone had ever called me that. I was flattered and somewhat suspicious. Who thinks like that?

Innocent men from small towns, I surmised on my way out the door.

At Donella's Organic Desserts in downtown Palm Beach, I selected a half-dozen delicious-looking lemon tarts and a box of citrus-persimmon tea leaves that would need to be brewed according to some complicated directions. I was no expert on preparing tea as I preferred coffee. But a tea ceremony for the lovers' reunion seemed so romantic, it had become a must-do. We'd have cocktails afterward. Or not, depending on how the afternoon's events turned out.

When I stepped out of the bakery, the sun splashed across the cobblestones, and I pulled on my shades. That's when I spotted a familiar figure less than a block away. Todd was standing with his back to me in front of the cigar store. He had his arms around a young woman of indeterminate age. A skinny bleached blonde with a huge, unnatural bust. When he leaned down to kiss her, I stepped back inside the pastry shop.

That pig! And in public? So brazen he felt free to display to the whole town his affair with some cheap little whore?

Sucking in my breath, I stepped outside again and marched down the street. Todd was standing alone, the girl walking east as he gazed after her.

"Friend of yours?" I asked him.

He jumped a little, then grinned down at me. His tennis whites were blinding in the noontime sun. "A little friend of Jeffrey Getzstein," he said with a louche expression on his handsome face. "I think she may be eighteen, but I'm not sure."

He seemed to think this was funny. I scowled at

him.

"We got back the other night," he continued, ignoring my obvious disapproval. "Great trip. Come over tonight, we can show you the photos."

Just what I wanted to do. Sit around with a couple of cheaters, looking at the pictures they took while traveling the world, hating on each other.

I stomped away. Todd called after me, "What'd I say?"

I think he was truly puzzled by my behavior.

When the cab let me off at Doyle's, I barely recognized the place. The grass was like a clean green sheet and all the trees had haircuts. Everything looked so different without the cover of fronds and bloom. The property appeared close shaved.

As I hurried up the flagstone walkway without any shade to protect me from the sun, the sky instantly darkened. Gray thunderclouds moved in fast, dousing the bright sunlight. Lightning blitzed the yard, swift as a struck match.

I made it to Doyle's doorway just as the deluge arrived, rain dumping from the black sky in torrents. We needed the rain. It had been a dry summer. But did it have to come down so hard? Today of all days?

But this was typical South Florida. One minute you're frying in the sun, the next you're drenched.

Doyle pulled me inside and relieved me of the groceries. I started to follow him into the kitchen but stopped short when I noticed the floral displays.

"Oh my god. What did he do?" I asked Doyle with a choked laugh.

The house was so full of colorful and aromatic bouquets, it was like a funeral home. The air was thick and hot, cloyingly sweet.

"My air conditioner crapped out," Doyle moaned. "It's like a sauna in here. I feel like a wilting tomato plant."

"You look vine," I joked.

He managed to smile, but his brow was furrowed, and he had dark circles under his eyes. The poor man was a wreck.

I tried to reassure him. "We can call one of those places that send out a repairman twenty-four/seven. Besides, the lovebirds will only be here for a short while. Then he'll take her back to his place, don't you think?"

Doyle shrugged. "I have no idea. He's been over here three times already today, checking on things. The trees, the grass. The flowers. He moved my couch! His nervousness, his vulnerability, it's making me nuts."

I patted his cheek and leaned in for a light kiss. "The importance of this little rendezvous has gotten blown up to a ridiculous degree. We all need to calm down. Hell, when those two first met, everyone was as cool and laid back as can be."

Doyle unloaded the grocery bags on the kitchen counter, which was bare. Had Gary made Doyle put all the appliances away? How odd. It was like he was staging the bungalow for a realtor's open house or a movie set.

Doyle said over his shoulder, "That was then. This is now. And I have no idea how to make tea out of tea leaves." He held up the box and frowned at me. "Can't we just have G&Ts?"

I laughed. "You and I can. But I'll make a pot of tea for the lovers. We'll serve them a tray, then scoot.

You do have a tea set, right? And a tray?"

Doyle spent some time hunting down the tea set, which is a standard accessory in all proper Palm Beach homes. Including the ones you rent furnished. I stumbled around the kitchen, and soon enough I'd brewed up a pot and the room smelled fruity. I laid out the pastries on the silver platter that matched the teapot.

"Anyone mind if I put on some mood music?" Gary popped his head in the kitchen doorway.

Doyle started, and I let out a small scream.

We laughed uncomfortably while Gary apologized. He was wildly overdressed in a pair of white flannel slacks with a yellow silk shirt and a pair of weird-looking white loafers. His hair was slicked back, his key lime cologne much too strong. I wanted to reach over and mess him up a little, make him back into the cool bartender Rose had fallen in love with. But, of course, that was then, as Doyle had pointed out. And this was…ridiculous.

As Doyle left the kitchen to assist with the musical arrangements, he rolled his eyes at me. I lifted an eyebrow as if to say, "*The kids are crazy. What can we do?*"

The rain had been drumming loudly on the Spanish tile roof, but by the time the tea was ready, it was only drizzling. The three of us sat stiffly in the living room, staring at the Persian rug. An antique grandfather clock struck four, and we looked at one another hopelessly.

Doyle was right. Gary's anxiety was permeating the house.

"Can we all just relax?" I said.

Gary's expression was a strange mix of disgust and animal fear. He jumped up and began pacing. He didn't stop moving, but he finally started talking.

"She's not coming. She chickened out, just like she did when I asked her to run away with me. Back when she loved me and not him. Todd. She's different now, I'm sure of it. I never should have done this. Made all the arrangements. Put everything on the line like this."

Doyle stood up, blocked Gary, and laid an arm across the other man's shoulder. "My cousin is a woman of her word. If she made other plans or something came up, she'd have called me. Or Coral. She's coming, so stop fidgeting."

Gary looked at Doyle, his wan face a mask of horror. "You don't understand. Everything I've done over the past five years has been to win her back. The deals I made, the people I allowed into my life? The overwrought estate next door, all those senseless parties? All of it, *all of it* was to attract Rose's attention. To make her see I am a man of means, a successful man who can provide for her in the way she's used to. After all I've done, what if she…"

He let the unthinkable remain unspoken.

Yeah, I thought, what if she decides she doesn't want him anymore?

But what I said was, "Give her a chance to get to know you again. Be yourself and see how that works. It worked quite well the last time."

His expression now was a combination of blatant disbelief and bottomless despair.

The doorbell rang.

I stood up. "Doyle and I will let her in. You wait here."

Gary shook himself like a frightened dog. He darted into the kitchen.

Doyle and I looked at each other.

"Whoa," he whispered.

I took his arm, and we walked through the vestibule to the front door. Rose stood on the stoop, her back to us. She was wearing a white cotton dress dotted with tiny pink hearts, and her hair was pinned up on her head. A misty sunlight filtered through the wet green of the yard and the sheer white of her outfit.

She turned to us, her face as sweet and innocent as her outfit. "Is this where you live, dear Doyle? It's like a fairytale cottage in the woods."

When she grabbed my hand, I noticed her wedding ring had been removed, and in its place was a silver band covered with tiny red stones. Garnets. I'd seen the ring in her special box. Gary had given it to her as an engagement ring before he left for the war. That day in her bedroom closet, I read the letters he'd sent her. Desperate, pleading letters reminding her of their promises and begging her to wait for his return.

"So where is he?" she said as we led the way inside the little house. "Or am I the first to arrive? I thought I'd be fashionably late." She smiled weakly. "I think I'm a bit of a mess. Nerves."

She followed us to the living room and sank quickly onto the velveteen couch. Her knees were shaking, poor girl. While I poured her a cup of tea, Doyle went into the kitchen to retrieve Gary.

The doorbell rang again.

Had Gary fled out the back, in order to pretend he'd just arrived? I hid my smile and went back to pouring tea.

Doyle answered the door and I heard low voices.

Rose stared at me, her face a sheet of starched

white cotton. "Oh my god."

Gary walked in, shoulders hunched, hands clasped behind his back, facial expression somber, dark. Like he was about to face a firing squad. He marched over and stood before Rose, who stared up at him with a look of childlike wonder on her face. Her hands shook so much I felt the need to relieve her of her teacup, which I did in the ensuing silence.

My nervous excitement got the better of me, and I lunged for a lemon tart, blurting, "Donatella makes the best pastries in town. And they're organic." I ate the entire thing in one bite while standing up, wolfing it down as I watched Gary and Rose marvel at one another in a brittle silence.

Doyle took me by the arm before I could say anything else stupid. "Come on, Coral. I need to show you something," he said in a commanding voice that translated to *we are outta here.*

He dragged me to the kitchen while I choked down the thick mass of rich dessert. "I need a drink." My voice was lemon clogged. What a fool, chugging pastry!

"You need to come out back with me and relax," Doyle instructed, grabbing a bottle of gin and two glasses from a cabinet shelf.

I followed him outside. The drizzle was heavy, so we stood under a thick banyan tree while he poured us each a hefty shot.

"Sorry about the lack of mixer," he said, "but I had to get out of there. The tension was too much." He clinked glasses with me. "Here's to love."

But he didn't appear to mean it. He had a sour expression, as if already disappointed in the afternoon's events. Such as they were.

"What's wrong?" I asked. "I think it's all going to work out." I fired down the shot. It burned a hole in the plug of dough and sugar in my throat, scorching its way to my gut. I felt instantly better, more easily able to maintain a groundless optimism. "They looked happy to see each other, right?"

Doyle's frown deepened. "Oh, I don't know. How much better off will she be with Gary than she is with Todd? Rich, power-mad factories of testosterone, both of them."

This was a surprise. "Why are you suddenly off Gary? I thought you loved the guy. You flew with him, played tennis, golf. You told me numerous times you think he's an awesome dude. Meanwhile, Todd is a boor and a hound dog. Gary is the one with all the class and good manners. And I believe he worships Rose."

Doyle had slugged his shot, too, so he poured us each another. "I'm sure he thinks he does. Because he isn't married to her. Todd, on the other hand, is. Married. To her. Rose."

Now he was stumbling over his words. Was he hiding something from me? I couldn't figure it. What had changed his mind so suddenly?

"Whatever has gotten into you, Doyle?" I set my glass on the fat bough of the tree we were sheltering under. It was as flat as a table and rough barked, like an old man with a life-toughened shell. "If you wanted to protect Rose, we should never have arranged this little tea party."

He looked at me sharply. "I'm not trying to protect Rose. I'm worried about Gary."

Aha.

The male bond, stronger than blood.

Doyle continued. "The guy has done things, unspeakable things, to get here. What he had to do to evolve from a law school dropout, a bartender, a war veteran, into the kind of man who lives here, in Palm Beach? You have no idea. He gave up his *soul* for that woman. I'm just hoping she doesn't spit it right out."

I sipped my drink. I wanted to be able to say, "*She won't. Rose would never do that.*" But I couldn't. After all, I'd seen her reject true love for comfort and status once before. Why wouldn't she do it again? Just because he was rich now didn't mean he would be her top choice. Gary Blass had work to do. He would need to convince Rose the life he was offering was the one she'd always dreamed of.

The question in my mind was this. *What if she already had the life she'd always wanted?*

Rose was beautiful, generous, a delight. She was my best friend in a mean, hard world. But I didn't know her. Not really.

And neither did Gary.

Chapter Seven
In the Midnight Zone

When thunder roared and lightning lit up the sky in jagged streaks, Doyle ushered us back inside. The clock in his living room was striking five when we peeked our heads in. Gary and Rose were seated at opposite ends of the long couch, staring at one another like a pair of tomcats. Electricity filled the warm air of the room.

She had tears on her face. Her amber eyes glistened, and her mouth looked bruised.

He was glowing. The man was absolutely radiant. "I'd like to show Rose around my place. Come with us," he instructed without taking his eyes off his prize.

Doyle looked at me, and I shrugged. Why not?

We went outside. The rain had stopped completely, and the sun peered out again from the heavy clouds. Rainbows spilled down from the gray thundercloud sky.

We traipsed across the damp yard, shortcutting through the freshly mowed grass, our feet and ankles getting soaked. Gary led the way. He was joyful and walked with an exuberant step, the pied piper of love. And money. Ahead of us, his pink manse sparkled in the burnt orange light of the late afternoon sun. It looked like a birthday cake baked specially for a ten-year-old girl.

As we passed by the gardens, Rose admired the fragrant flowers.

"I planted the rose bushes just for you," Gary teased.

Or was he serious? There was almost an acre of bushes. Roses in every hue from white to cream, pale yellow to golden peach, coral and magenta, hot pink and fire engine red.

By the time we got to the front door, my shoes squeaked and squished. So I kicked them off, leaving them on the landing. Rose laughed and did the same with her damp ballet slippers. In our bare feet, we wandered through the immense marble foyer to the carpeted hallways, then up and down the polished oak staircases, skipping like schoolgirls from room to shining room. I watched Gary's face as he pointed out his museum pieces to Rose, the artwork by famous names, the artifacts from world travels. I could see he was evaluating their worth based on her reactions to them.

He saved the library for last. When we all stood outside the tall doors, Rose said, "I don't see how you live here all alone."

"I don't intend to keep it that way," he answered her. "But in the meantime, I fill it up with all sorts of interesting people."

Interesting, maybe. All sorts, definitely. All ages might be the better description. Including under the legal age.

He pushed through the door and held it open for us to file inside.

When Rose saw the bookshelves covering the walls, she gasped. "Why, this is incredible," she said, tears clouding her eyes. "This is the most beautiful home library I've ever seen. I could live in this room."

Gary's chest swelled. He pointed to me. "I have all of Coral's aunt's books. On the shelf where I keep my favorite novels."

Tears popped into my eyes as well. How sweet. My aunt was successful, yes. She had made a name for herself and a fortune with her writing. But her books were dime store romances. Trashy fairytales. Junk food fiction. Everyone knew that. Yet Gary had filed her collection next to books by Hemingway, Faulkner, and Fitzgerald. For me, he'd done that for me. Because Rose loved me.

Through the arched windows overlooking the backyard, we watched as the rain started up again. The pool water spluttered, and ripples formed on the surface reflection of marching gray clouds.

Gary seated himself on the corner of his desk and stared out. "When the day is clear, I can see your house perfectly from here. Like it's been framed just for me. Which is why this room is my favorite," he said to Rose.

She walked over to stand beside him. He slid an arm around her slim waist, and she kissed the top of his head.

Doyle took my hand. "I'm going to drive Coral home so she can get some work done. Do you need a lift, Cuz?"

Cuz? Doyle never called her that.

Rose wiped the tears from her face. She was staring at Gary and saying nothing. In a love trance, apparently.

"I'll see to it she gets home safely," Gary said, his voice thick with barely withheld emotion.

"We can see ourselves out then. So, ah, see you

folks later," Doyle said.

They didn't seem to hear, so lost were they in one another's eyes. The energy in the room was pulsating, the air throbbed with eroticism and animal heat. They were possessed by an intensity I had never felt in my life, I was sure of it.

Wow.

Outside in the now heavy rain, I slid into my soggy shoes. We walked back to Doyle's place, yielding to the drenching we were receiving. I was so caught up in what had happened, the images of the reunited lovers flashing through my mind like a romance film, that I didn't even care I was getting soaked, that by the time I got home I would be wet straight through to my skin.

"Looks like those two are happy with each other," I bubbled, happy for the moment myself.

Above us in the damp trees, birds rustled, their burbling song clear and pleasant, a sign the rain would soon end. Again.

I took Doyle's hand. He squeezed mine in return, said something I didn't understand at the time. "Yes, but only until they realize the colossal vitality of their shared illusion."

Doyle O'Henry, a banker with a philosopher's depth of understanding of human behavior. And he was right. Because it was true. Happiness is but a moment in time, fleeting and inexplicable. For all of us, a little blessing that, like a hard rain, like the warming sunshine, like the sweet song of a cardinal or bluebird, never lasts as long as we might wish.

****

Doyle dropped me off at the guest cottage, and I hurried inside. I stripped off all my clothes and jumped in a steaming hot shower. Then I wrapped myself in a flannel throw. I was still chilled, so I drank a glass of apricot brandy while I lounged on the sofa.

What a day. First, I'd spotted Todd laying a raunchy smooch on that too-busty, too-young chick. That was just so weird I had yet to tell anyone about it. Then came Gary and his bizarre case of first-date nerves, his strange behavior while waiting for Rose to arrive for tea. Followed by his startling transformation after they spent an hour alone together. What had Rose told him to puff him up so? And what would happen next? Would they run off somewhere? What about Penny? Would Rose take the baby with them? Or would Gary march across the Intracoastal bridge and confront Todd, order him to get lost, because he, Gary, had always been the man, the *only* man, for Rose?

When I imagined that little scene, I could actually see it unfolding the way it does in romance novels whenever a cheating spouse is denounced by a loyal defender. Often, there was bloodshed. Sometimes, the cheater died.

When I finished my brandy, I fell into bed and slept for ten hours.

In the morning when I awoke, refreshed and filled with an immense, inexplicable optimism, I made a pot of strong coffee and began to write. This continued for hours, then days.

****

I didn't see much of Doyle over the next few weeks. This was partly due to my sudden and overwhelming need to be alone so I could focus on my—finally—steadily progressing work. Which was really coming together, much to my surprise. But Doyle had backed off as well. He wasn't calling me either. I was too engrossed in my research notes and expanding thesis draft to wonder why.

Rose dropped by every now and then to update me on what had become her sizzling hot affair. She reeked of illicit sex and feminist freedom, attributes I found rather fetching. She even dressed differently, her pure white outfits replaced by short denim skirts, colorful stretch tops and flip-flops. Penny accompanied her often on her secret outings, which she drove to herself, making me wonder whether her sexy driver had been fired. I reminded myself to ask Rose about him, then forgot. Whenever I saw her, our conversation focused on her deep and life-changing passion and Gary's reciprocal fervor.

My feelings for Doyle began to lose steam. Without meaning to, I had reevaluated our affair under the revealing spotlight of Rose and Gary's big love. Our feelings, as insipid as they seemed in comparison, were judged inadequate.

But in the long run, this was a good thing. I worked hard, drank little, ran daily, ate and slept well, and was highly productive. Before I lost steam, I clocked thousands of words on the thesis draft, which translated to hundreds of pages. And then, suddenly, I had nothing more to say.

It was late morning in early September when I wandered across the backyard looking for Rose. I found her sprawled on a beach chair in the sun. Her brown limbs gleamed with oily suntan lotion, her nose and cheeks an unpleasant shade of pink.

I stood over her. "What the hell, Rose. Your face is burning."

She opened her eyes and smiled at me, languidly, from behind her rose-colored department store shades. "Don't worry about me, Coco. How's your work coming along?"

I dragged an umbrella table next to her and sat in its shade. "How about some sunblock for your face? I can fetch mine." With my skin, I always had a tube on hand.

She sat up and crossed her slick legs. "I'm timing it carefully. I've only been out here for a short while. I'll be fine." She reached over to pat my hand. "I hear your keyboard clacking like mad whenever I come up to the front door, so I just leave you be. I don't want to interrupt. You're making real progress, aren't you?"

Her happiness for me was so loving it brought tears to my eyes. I wanted to be happy for her as well, so I asked about her most recent outings.

She held a finger to her lips, then nodded to the dock. "Let's go down and catch the breeze."

We walked down to the deck chairs facing the water, where the home security cameras would not reach. I wasn't sure if she was under surveillance or just being paranoid, but I was pretty sure she wasn't too far off the mark. Todd was controlling in so many ways. Why not keep a close eye on his home and family?

"My heart is in a constant, turbulent riot," she said, her face devoid of expression. "I saw Todd with his latest girl. She's pretty but very young. And so…common."

I pretended not to know who she was referring to. Perhaps I didn't. He might have had a whole clubhouse full of young girls. "What girl?"

She shook her head. Her hair was longer, fuller.

She'd lightened it so that the honey blonde was now streaked with sunny highlights. "Her name is Brittney. He leased a condo in town where he meets with her in the afternoon when she gets out of school." She turned to me, her eyes unreadable behind the pink shades. "*High* school. She's a *senior*."

I didn't know what to say. I wondered if the girl was of age, or if he'd crossed the line into criminal behavior. "Did he tell you all this?"

"No, I hired a private investigator to spy on him and prepare a report. I'm sure he's doing the same thing with me," she said. "Giving the divorce attorneys all the ammo they'll need for the big showdown. My reputation is totally ruined."

She wiped a tear from one eye. When I brushed a gentle hand across her shoulder she flinched. "Geez, Coco, you're right. I got too much sun. Already!" She moaned dramatically.

I took off my tee shirt and gave it to her. She put it on carefully. I sat there in my sports bra and running shorts, waiting for her to continue.

Because there was more. There was *always* more with these things. More hurt, more ugliness, more dishonesty and betrayal. For the first time, I wondered whether her affair with Gary was just a revenge fling. For his sake, I hoped not.

"I don't know what to do. I want to make Gary happy, but he's putting on the pressure. He wants me to renounce my entire history with Todd. He wants me to tell my husband I never loved him, to say to Todd's face I only loved *him*. Gary." She gulped at the air. "I don't know. It seems so harsh. And is it even true? Have I only loved Gary all this time?"

Was she asking me to answer that? In the moment, I doubted she'd want to hear what I had to say. I'd seen her when they returned from their two-year fantasy island honeymoon. She was heartbroken that he'd been unfaithful, but it sure looked as if she'd forgiven his trespasses.

On my occasional visits, I watched her as she silently begged for his casual glance, the smallest touch, desperate for any reassuring words, meaningless as they might be. She followed him around like a duckling, imprinting him on her brain, her tender heart. Typical wife of an abuser, she kept asking for it, and the more he kicked her, the harder she worshipped him. Or so it had seemed to me until this past spring when the baby arrived.

After that, I noticed with relief how her passion had cooled. She was less needy and much less desirous. He went his own way, and she appeared…relieved. Angry when he failed to cover up his digressions, but not so wounded. Not so battered.

And then Gary appeared, like a fairytale prince ready to rescue the sad princess from her self-imposed prison.

But I said nothing, let her keep talking it through.

"I love my life, you know that, Coral. But what if he keeps going after girls? *Young* girls? I can't allow that. I have to move on."

This I agreed with. "So, do. File for divorce. Do it before he does, then fight for what's yours. You can start over with Penny. You'll be awarded a fair amount of economic support from Todd. He won't be able to shirk his financial responsibilities. Besides, he has so much money, he'll probably opt to be very generous with you."

Todd was one of those men who, by the time they reach an advanced middle age, were paying alimony and child support all over town.

She shook her head. "Maybe not. In Florida, you have to be married longer than we've been to get half your spouse's assets. We've only been married for five years."

I was starting to get thirsty. I'd need a drink soon. "So who needs half? He's incredibly wealthy. Settle for a million or two, then go back to college. Finish your degree, get a cool job, explore your own life. You married him so young, Rosie. It's not too late to restart your life as an independent woman."

She looked at me as if I were out of my mind. "No way! I'm not going to do *that.* I'm going to marry Gary. As soon as my divorce is final. He's promised to take care of me and Penny. We'll move over there." She pointed to the mansion across the waterway. Her tears had dried, and she smiled, her rosebud nose twitching like a little bunny's. In that moment, I thought she was equally adorable and about as dumb. "I love that house," she said in a high-pitched girl's voice. "The library is to die for."

She had no idea of the reality of her unreality, the vulnerability of her hazy cotton ball illusions. I didn't know the extent of the problem either, not yet, but I was pretty sure something wasn't right in glitzy Palm Beach. Todd's affair with a high school girl, for example. All those kids at Gary's parties, the half-dressed teenagers flirting with the rich old men in suit jackets, those heavy, jowled men with a taste for hard booze and saturated fat. And all the male celebrities who turned up without their female partners. What exactly was going on?

I thought about Doyle's client, the infamous Jeffrey Getzstein, Palm Beach socialite and predator extraordinaire. What if he was in business with Gary? Was Getzstein involved in the parties, the old men and young girls that rubbed up against one another every weekend? Was this a primary source for the seedy underbelly of extreme wealth? It seemed quite likely.

Right then, staring across the Intracoastal at the birthday cake mansion on its bright green tray of lush landscape, I decided I would make a point of finding out who Gary Blass really was. Maybe I could dig up some credible dirt on the great Getzstein while I was at it. And on Todd. In fact, I made another vow. I would learn exactly what was going down in Palm Beach. Before Rose stepped in another pile of shit that had been shined to look like gold.

Fool's gold.

I loved her. She would always be my bestie. So even if she did not believe it was essential to protect herself and her daughter, I did.

Besides, investigating the transgressors of Palm Beach was much more appealing than sitting at my computer with my mouth open to a silent scream. Since I'd hit another thesis roadblock, I needed a detour. A search for the gory details on some of the many local scandals seemed as good as any.

Chapter Eight
In the Abyss

Within a few days, I believed everything and nothing I'd ever heard about Gary Blass. Because enough reliable information to form an accurate history of the man's life was nowhere to be found. It was as if he'd been shot out of a cannon from nowhere and landed here, smack in the middle of Palm Beach high society. No online accounts of his education, his military service, his work history. No candid photos illustrating his rise to the high-income bracket. He had no past, none that I could find. No attendance record at Suffolk Law, no service honors, no social media accounts. And his present consisted of what you saw was what you got—grand displays of excessive wealth from ineffable sources and over-the-top weekend parties he didn't bother to attend.

After hours spent on my laptop running down dead-ends, I quit. Gary must have, at some point, adopted a false identity. I would need to get a look at some of his private papers and see if they held any clues to his true identity. But how?

In the meantime, I trolled closer to home. The sour juice on Todd was all too easy to find. He left a sticky trail that led from his estate directly to his lair. He was indeed fooling around with a cheerleader from Palm Beach High. But with a bit of in-person spying, local gossip, and social media stalking, I discovered his slinky little Brittney was really a hustler from the projects. Her recent breast enlargement surgery had been paid for by a mystery donor, which was weird. Also, when she wasn't shacking up with Todd, she spent time at a ramshackle apartment complex on the very wrong side of the tracks, where a crew of biker brothers and distant cousins waited anxiously for her to score big with a rich rube in Palm Beach.

It's amazing what one can discover skulking about.

Jeffrey Getzstein's history was a mixed bag. I found a lot of articles on his philanthropy, his donations to university research centers, his mega real estate holdings. Not much else was available online, however. Like what was he doing to amass all that wealth? Unknown. He kept a pretty low profile for an infamous billionaire with an address book full of celebs.

As I ran to the beach every morning, sweat dripping, limbs heavy from the heat, I thought about my quest. For the dirt on Gary and Getzstein, I would have to go deep. In person, not online.

This appealed so much more than working on my thesis.

I began hanging around the local bars in the early afternoons. There were quite a few in town, but what I wanted was an upscale den for blackout drunks. Locals who knew the dirty lowdown and were too soused to keep it quiet.

Sitting at the gleaming oak bar at The Horned Owl, I learned more than I needed to know about the two men in question, plus much more than I wanted to know about my own doomed love. I'd added his name to the list of questionable men after stumbling across some very unpleasant facts online.

As it turned out, Doyle O'Henry was a cheat too, a milk-fed liar. Facebook gleefully informed me that he'd left a cute little fiancée back in Bumfuck, North Dakota. A dental hygienist named Lauren, who couldn't wait until he returned so they could start their family.

"We already have the names picked out for our first three babies," she cooed to all her FB friends.

When I read that, my poor heart sank down to my uterus. I had to float it back up with a tall glass of lukewarm California Cabernet at The Owl.

The lowlife louse. And I'd thought he kind of loved me.

Once hatred burned in my gut—or was that the cheap wine?—I looked for more reasons to abhor him. And the hollow-eyed regulars were only too happy to oblige. After all, Doyle worked for the scummiest bastard in town. So I asked my bar mates about Doyle's number one client, wondering aloud why nobody turned in the great man to the FBI. The entire town of Palm Beach knew Getzstein was running a teenybopper sex ring, for god's sake.

An inebriated woman dressed in a gold lamé skirt suit sat on the stool beside me, downing gimlets. "Darling girl," she said in a nicotine-scarred voice. "Palm Beach eats its own. But we never squeal on each other. Never."

Randy the bartender, a jacked surfer dude around my age, agreed. "The cops are on Jeffrey's payroll anyway. So are the local councilmen. And it only goes up from there."

The gimlet lady uncrossed her bony legs and

leaned toward me. She was old, or maybe she just looked it because the booze had vacuumed her out. Her breath was like formaldehyde. "My dear, Jeffrey will never be punished for his peccadillos. He has way too much leverage."

An elderly gent in a wrinkled wool vest chimed in. "Man's not the only one in town with that kind of resume."

Everyone laughed. Except me. My hometown was even more corrupt than I'd thought. Financial crimes, of course. Tax evasion, offshore laundering, they all did it. But letting teenagers get manhandled by a pervert? I would've put it past them. Past anybody.

Silly me.

I wondered how much Rose knew about Getzstein and his possible connection to Gary. I didn't dare ask. I so desperately wanted to keep believing in her. If I didn't, I'd have no one to believe in but myself, which I was struggling with at the moment.

I was disgusted with my own appalling sentimentality. What kind of juvenile claptrap had I been telling myself? Love and romance? What hogwash. This world is nothing but illusion and grift. We see those flashing lights that look green but, when you open your eyes wide enough, you can see they are blood-red.

As red as another glass of bad wine.

****

Recovering from long days of barfly duty, I was nursing a nauseating hangover on the sofa on a warm Friday afternoon in September when my phone buzzed. Doyle.

I had yet to tell him I knew his shit and the jig was

up, which was fortunate because I needed him to help me uncover the truth about Gary. So I had decided I would have to play Doyle for a while. Kind of like he'd been playing me.

"Hey there," I answered in a sexy growl. I was hoping that would help soothe him while he accused me of ignoring his recent texts and emails. "Miss me?"

"I did," he said. "I got back to town Sunday night and was hoping to see you. Where've you been?"

I concocted a long tale about imaginary deadlines for an invented magazine editor who was absolutely salivating while waiting for me to submit a draft of one section of my sure-to-be-a-major-world-changer thesis.

He listened patiently, then said, "Come over, Coral. We can fool around."

The bile charged up my throat. The bastard. He'd been distant for weeks, and now I was supposed to just smile and lay down? Where had *he* been lately? He claimed he'd been in Manhattan on business for Getzstein, but had he really? Or had he run home to Bumfuck to play family dentist with Lauren?

When my ire died down, I felt like I might throw up. Maybe he *had* gone to New York, but was he there to party with his twisted client? Had Doyle indulged in teenyboppers, too? Was he that bad, that different from the man I believed I'd been seeing? He was a liar and a cheat, so what other digressions was he capable of?

All of them.

I swallowed the previous night's booze barf crawling up my throat. With great effort, I managed to lie. "Okay, but let's hang out at Gary's tonight. I feel like partying."

Of course, I surely didn't. But I did feel like spying

on Gary. And, after a full month without the usual weekend party at the Blass mansion, Gary had suddenly announced his intention to host a big blowout. Why, nobody seemed to know. He'd quit giving away the booze soon after he reunited with his true love. So why was he starting up the party train again?

Despite my sleuthing, Gary remained enigmatic. His real estate holdings, too, were unclear. The LLC that held the mortgage on his property was a dead-end. I couldn't track down the face behind the deed. At the local bars, nobody had any solid facts on the man. But everyone had at least one outrageous story they were just dying to share.

Gary worked for the CIA and had been stationed in the Middle East.

He ran guns to Ukraine and Sudan.

He worked on Russian oil rigs, in Chinese coal mines, deep sea mining.

He invented a surefire cure for the hangover.

He founded a dating website, and his startup went public.

He was on the board of Facebook but quit Silicon Valley because his nerves were shot.

Oh, and he moved to Palm Beach because his old flame lived here and he wanted to woo her back. Everyone agreed on that one.

Including me.

But I kept silent. Let them talk, I was there to listen. And to spy.

On the phone that day, I kept my cool and flirted with Doyle, convincing him to go to Gary's with me. He didn't sound enthusiastic, but he didn't say no either. After we caught up with one another's bullshit stories over a few free drinks, I would ditch him. My plan was to rifle through whatever papers I could find in Gary's library. I wanted to see if I could uncover something solid, facts about the man that could lead me to the truth.

Doyle and I settled on a time for me to come by. He was probably thinking he'd make love to me from behind while continuing to lie to my face, pretending to be the honest Midwesterner with a true north moral compass.

Not tonight, big boy, I thought with a painful grin.

"See you then," I promised, sounding as excited and horny as possible.

When we hung up, I realized my heart was pounding. With shame and disgust? Fear and loathing? No, my pulse jumped with actual excitement. Not about seeing that lying skunk, Doyle. No, I was excited because the night ahead promised me a delicious taste of espionage. Most thrilling was knowing I was uncovering the truth about these dirtbags, these cheating Palm Beach men. Seemingly upstanding citizens, wealthy snobs hiding who they really were behind a gold wall. Behind the thinnest palette of gilded lies, mind games, and terrible secrets.

Rose called next, asking if Doyle and I were going to the party. When I said yes, she said she would drive us there. That sounded good to me. I could use her as a distraction to keep Doyle at a distance while at his place. Then she would keep Gary busy while I ransacked his library.

Rose was out of breath, as if she'd been exerting herself. This was out of character, but I didn't ask. It was enough that we would go to Gary's together. She didn't have any idea what I was up to, nor would she have approved. She was still blindly, madly in love. She wasn't looking for truth.

But the truth could change things and spin them in a whole new direction. And my heart told me it would do exactly that.

****

Rose knocked on my door promptly at nine. She was going to drive as the limo was no longer in use. The sexy Latino was gone. She hadn't wanted the help to know what she was up to on her excursions to see Gary.

Due to my lack of interest in Doyle's affections, I had dressed down. I didn't want to look sexy. I wanted to look like I felt—disinterested. Besides, I needed to slink around the party unobserved. Like a wallflower, the old maid nobody notices.

But when I answered the door, Rose was not pleased. She gave me the judgmental girlfriend onceover and snapped, "Where do you think we're *going?* A rummage sale?"

I smirked. "Funny. I have a wee headache, so I didn't—"

Her frown deepened, her voice dropping to a low growl. "You are *not* backing out of this, my friend. And I am *not* going with you looking like that. Do you know what kind of monumental fiction I had to invent to get a night away from this place? It's like a fucking jail cell living with that man, and tonight is my ticket to freedom. But if you're not with me, then the whole goddam story falls apart."

My mouth dropped open. Rose acting pissy, bitchy, and swearing like a mule driver? Whoa. What was up with her?

I backed into the living room and spun around, heading for the bedroom. "Help yourself to some vino. The bottle's on the counter. Maybe it will kill the bug you've got up your ass," I said over my shoulder.

She snorted.

I moved to the closet. I would do what she wanted. I would dress to please her. Then she would tell me what she was really upset about. Something was up, I was sure of it.

I heard the sound of Cab hitting a glass. Then she appeared in the doorway, full goblet in hand, and watched me undress. Her eyes were like slits. She looked like a sleepy cat. Was she *stoned?*

"Are you fucking high?" I asked her, sliding into a pair of white slacks that could use an iron but were at least clean. "You're acting very un-dude, dude."

She managed a half smile. "Sorry. I'm at the end of it. If I have to sit across the dinner table from that man one more night, I just… I can't do it anymore, Coco. I have to leave him."

Using my palms, I pressed the wrinkles from a rayon blouse and tucked it into my pants.

Rose shook her head. "Untucked," she ordered, so I complied.

While I pulled a battered jewelry box out of the top drawer of the bureau and selected a pair of fake jade earrings and matching necklace, I said, "Okay, I get it."

In the mirror, I held up my jewelry and our eyes met.

She nodded, approving.

"So are you leaving him *tonight*?" I asked.

My voice shook a little. So did my hands when I

poked the earrings through the piercings in my earlobes. Why were we speaking so freely if Todd had the place wired?

She gulped her wine. Then she said, "You aren't supposed to know this. Nobody is. Gary and I are going to run away. Tonight, while his party is in full swing, we're going to slip off. I'll send for Penny once we get established." She tsked. "Palm Beach is no place for a child to grow up. It warps the personality."

She had that right. Look at me. Look at her.

I struggled with the necklace clasp. "So what am I supposed to tell Todd when he comes over here looking for you? Because he will. You know that."

Her face was a mask of relaxed acceptance. Her eyes darted, though, skittering. "You're a fucking dog with a bone, Coco. Just go hang out at Doyle's for the weekend. By the time you come back on Monday, we'll be far enough away that Todd can't do anything about it. I'll call him then, let him know I won't be staying in the marriage, which he probably already knows, the devious fucker."

Rose never cursed like this. I shivered. Was I afraid for her? Or of Todd's anger, his recriminations? I guessed both. But not enough to avoid him by staying at Doyle's. I would come home after I finished my spy caper and, if necessary, face the irate cuckolded husband.

But I didn't tell Rose this. I avoided her eyes by attempting to brush some of the snarls out of my knotted hair. While I fiddled with a tube of lipstick, she tried to seduce me into a code of sisterly silence. Her glass was almost empty.

"You can't tell him anything. Not a word. I'm

desperately sorry to leave you in this awkward position. You are the best person I know, Coco, and a loyal friend. You know how much Gary means to me. You of all people understand how urgent it is that I embark on the life I really want. The life I need in order to truly live!"

Her face did not convey joy. She was scared, too.

I promised her I would do as she asked. But I was lying. I had other ideas. I intended to find out who Gary really was and what kind of life he might provide for her. Here in his Palm Beach estate, he sure looked the part, but was it all an act to win back her love and trust? Once he whisked her away from her husband and child, her family and the life she'd always known, would the foundation he'd erected to impress her crumble, revealing the poor and sandy Florida dirt?

I had no idea.

But neither did Rose.

She came up behind me, and our eyes met in the mirror again. "You'll bear the brunt of his wrath, I'm afraid. But really, Todd's harmless. All bluster, no bite. Tell him you don't know where I am, which will be true because I won't tell you where we're going."

She stroked my hair, patting it into place around my face. I could see in her strained smile how desperate she was for my approval. My blessing.

"You might want to move in with Doyle for a while. Maybe rent your own cottage, if you plan to stick around town for the winter," she said. "It was so wonderful having you nearby. Just like the old days. Once Gary and I get settled, we'll have you to our place for future writing retreats."

Her smile was as phony as the gemstones in my art

fair jewelry. I looked away, searching the room for my phone, my keys, my purse. My embarrassment for her was excruciating. I don't believe I'd ever before felt such a profound sense of humiliation for someone else.

"Let's get going," I said. "My headache is getting worse."

I was worried I might unearth the most unspeakable truth at Gary's. That I might have to stop her from running away with him. There are fifty ways to leave your husband and child, and this didn't seem like one of them. Too much was still unknown.

She managed to grab me and kiss me on the cheek on our way to the door. "You are my bestie, Coco," she said. "I love you."

"Love you, too," I responded.

I loved her so much I was about to perform a B&E in order to save her.

Chapter Nine
The Haldal

We drove across the Intracoastal bridge in silence. A full moon lit the way, shining a brilliant spotlight on the quiet black water. I rolled down the window. The air had a touch of autumn to it, slightly drier and quite cool. I smelled smoke.

My mind was on overdrive. What secrets might I uncover at Gary's and could I share them with Rose in time? And why was she acting so carelessly, so unlike herself?

Distracted and amped up, I stared down at the ground on either side of the waterway. The embankments were lined with sleeping bags, the grassy strips full of milling people. I leaned out the window to get a better look. Bonfires in trash cans, gray wisps of ash wafting on the night air. People huddling, children running about. Dogs, even a few cats.

"It's getting cold up in Philly and Boston, New York City," Rose explained. "There's more of them camping out here every fall."

Just before the winter arrived, busloads of homeless people with one-way tickets to paradise pulled into terminals around South Florida on a daily basis. This had been the case for many years. During my youth, I had noted the occasional homeless person wearing a backpack or wheeling a shopping cart, wandering the streets. Now whole families lived in cardboard boxes and panhandled outside boutiques. Trash piled up in the parks, and sometimes human waste could be seen on the sidewalks.

Below us on both sides of the Intracoastal, the kids were playing tag. Someone strummed a guitar. The moonlight bounced off dozens of people, a vast sleepover party that would continue until the spring. Unless the city kicked them out of their encampment and forced them to go elsewhere, on to another temporary location where they would know they were equally unwelcome.

Seeing all the homeless people with nothing for themselves, for their children, for their future, was disquieting. Here I was, sitting in the passenger seat of a luxury car that cost enough to house most of those families for the entire winter while my fellow humans were down there desperately trying to survive. They had kids to feed and no money to provide for their basic needs while we traveled from one multi-million-dollar mansion full of waste and deceit to another.

But now was not the time to worry about the overwhelming inequity of the world. We were almost to Doyle's.

As she turned in his driveway, Rose remarked on the traffic ahead. A line of fancy cars snaked up the road to Gary's.

"Would you look at all that?" she exclaimed in obvious awe.

This annoyed me. "The wealthiest people will make a beeline for free booze," I said with a sneer.

She snorted, but I meant it.

After she parked the car, I followed her up the slate

walkway to the front door. There was a stiff breeze off the ocean, the air chilled, wintery. Hugging myself, I hung back, trying to think things through. I would have to accomplish my espionage quickly, before the two lovers split for wherever it was they were headed.

Doyle had left the door open, and soft yellow light spilled out. We stepped inside, and he appeared in the hallway, a martini glass in hand.

"My two favorite ladies," he said with a happy smile. "Come in, and we'll have a drink before we go drinking."

Rose laughed and rushed over to kiss him on both cheeks. I smiled, but the strain made my jaw ache. When he nuzzled my neck, it was all I could do not to vomit. He smelled like pine needles dipped in hot chocolate.

It sounds good, but it's not.

Rose and I took seats in his velvety armchairs while he made us martinis. He insisted we had to try them, a new recipe he claimed he'd just invented. I swallowed my bile and played along. Van Morrison was on the stereo, and I tried to lose myself in his lovely poetry.

Rose smiled at me, the gleam in her eyes full of unbridled joy. "I'm going to have a happy life," she said in a low voice, "with the man of my dreams."

For a fleeting moment, I believed her. She would soon experience romantic and spiritual fulfillment with her devoted partner, her beautiful child, and the kind of happiness that came with making the right choices in life.

But then Doyle arrived with a silver tray, on which sat three mud-brown martinis, and the idealistic hallucination faded away. Once again, I examined the facts of the matter with a cynical eye.

"Mocha martinis!" Doyle announced.

"Those look disgusting," I blurted.

Doyle and Rose laughed.

****

The plump moon sat higher in the sky, draped in a lacy shawl of wispy white clouds. The castoff moonlight was reflected in the shiny new model automobiles that led up the pebbled driveway to the Blass mansion. The wide lawn was clogged with cars, many of which probably belonged to the young drivers' parents. People who had no idea where their underage kids were drinking tonight.

As we climbed the stairs to Gary's front door, Rose marveled at the size of the crowd. People were spilling out of the house and loitering around the steps, the circular driveway, the topiary, and the central fountain. High school kids, mainly, standing in tight groups with their cigarettes and red plastic cups, their in-jokes and fake laughter. A fey fistfight broke out in a cadre of teenage boys dressed alike in polo shirts and sockless loafers. The girls scattered, spilling beer and squealing.

I checked for Rose's reaction to the kind of people Gary had hosted every weekend. Underage drinking was certainly not to be encouraged. It was by no means lawful. But Rose's smile was beatific. She remained smitten and therefore guileless, totally clueless. She did not see what was right in front of her.

But neither had I with Doyle. Perhaps we don't see the ugly truth so that love may bloom, babies will be created, and life on this troubled earth can go on.

Doyle suggested we avoid the knot of revelers

clogging the front entrance and travel through the side yard. I followed the two of them down the stairs again and around the side of the house. We ducked under the drooping fronds of cabbage palms and Christmas palms, fat poincianas with brick-red blooms. Tucked away out of the sea breeze, the night was perfectly warm, like a hand that held you gently as you swam though the darkness.

Security lights flashed on, spotlighting our approach as we walked alongside the house. I felt obvious in my intent, although rationally I knew this was silly. I had yet to make a move in any direction other than what looked like a beeline for the bars by the pool.

But Doyle stopped before we reached the backyard and ushered us in a side door. We went up a narrow set of stairs and passed through a sliver of a doorway to find ourselves standing between stacks in the library. *Ask and you shall receive*, I thought, holding back a bark of surprised laughter.

"He isn't here," Doyle said. "That's odd. Let's check out back."

I excused myself. "I need to find the powder room. I'll come find you after." I blew a kiss as I walked off and called out, "Grab me a finger bowl, will you, darling?"

Doyle nodded and smiled, his jade eyes full of what looked like adoration.

What an actor.

I turned away, feeling like I might be violently ill. Maybe it was the gross martini, but one thing was certain. I had to end the charade before I made myself physically sick.

The powder room was quaint, wallpapered with shiny floral bouquets and lined with shelves of tiny china figurines studded with jewels. These were the kind of knickknacks that could buy a homeless family a trailer to live in, maybe a townhome.

I examined myself in the mirror. My forehead was slick with sweat, my face pink and blotchy. Perhaps investigative work was best left to the professionals. I felt like I was going to have a goddamn stroke.

I laughed at myself, and that calmed me. I splashed a little cold water on my face and dried it with a decorative hand towel.

Get it together, Coral. Chill out, girl. Go in there and find something, I told myself.

Back in the library, I walked over to the glass desk, attempting to look like I was waiting for Gary. I figured there were security cameras secreted in the stacks. I would soon find out if a guard was manning them. I knew I had to make my moves subtle and swift.

The desktop was mostly clean with a paperweight and a solid gold pen set, a legal notepad and a landline phone. I stood there looking around casually, checking my watch, as if I had an appointment with the man and he was late.

On the legal pad in block letters, it read, *JG wants a delivery tonight.*

JG had to be Jeffrey Getzstein. He wanted a delivery from Gary, but of what? And who wrote the note? Gary, as a reminder? Or someone else, like Getzstein's girlfriend, perhaps? Probably. She was at every party I'd attended at Gary's. Maybe she was the messenger. So what did Gary provide for the great Getzstein? Girls? Drugs? Blackmail tapes of girls and drugs and rich old men who should've known better?

I stepped out of a shoe, then leaned over, pretending to remove a stone picked up on the pebbled driveway. Instead, I cracked open the lowest desk drawer, searching for something concrete. Delivery could mean anything. It didn't *have* to mean he wanted Gary to send him something criminal.

Or did it? I kept telling myself I wouldn't buy it until I saw the price tag.

And then I saw it.

In the deep bottom drawer, nestled beside a quart of Jack Daniels, a pair of beat down leather cowboy boots, and a serious looking handgun—passports. Two of them. One light blue. One dark red.

I slid one hand inside the drawer. Sucking in a ragged breath and holding it, I flipped open the blue passport and scanned it. Gary Blass, US citizen, a man who had traveled through much of the world, which made sense. Then I opened up the red one and squeaked out a tiny scream.

I almost didn't recognize him. In the yellowed mug shot, young Gary had a buzz cut and black-framed glasses. Name: Gavan Blazinskarov. Place of birth: Moscow. Citizenship: Russian.

My heart lunged into my throat so that I was choking. Coughing so hard my eyes teared up, I dropped the Russian passport as if it had spontaneously combusted, then quickly retrieved it, tucking it back where I'd found it. When I slammed the drawer shut, my thumb was in the way, and I cursed under my breath.

Mere seconds after I limped out from behind his desk, wiping my tears and still trying to look busy with my pebbled shoe, Gary—or should I say, Mr. Blazinskarov—entered the room. He stared at me for a moment, his piercing blue eyes questioning. Had he seen me snooping in his desk drawer? Had he been sitting in a security office somewhere, watching me betray his trust?

I held my breath, but to my surprised relief, his eyes softened, and he said, "Is she here?"

As I slid my foot back into my shoe, I knew he had instantly dismissed me from suspicion. Men. They think with their pricks. And in so doing, they underestimate the power of women to see past sex to something greater. Something far more dangerous.

I fake smiled. "She's outside looking for you. Shall we go find her?" I hooked my arm through his, hoping he wouldn't notice how badly my body was trembling.

He didn't appear to. Perhaps because he was a nervous wreck himself. "Did she tell you?" he asked in a voice as frightened as a child's. "About our plan for tonight?"

"A little," I said. "Just enough to survive the third degree from her husband."

He hugged me close. "I will always be grateful to you, Coral. I doubt Rose would have the courage to do this without your support."

My heart sank into my upset gut and sat there, a brooding stone. I'd encouraged her to abandon her cushy life of leisure, new motherhood, and top-shelf prosperity in one of the prettiest, wealthiest places in the country. And for what, to be with *this* man? A liar, a sham, and who knew what else?

He might be a real honest-to-goodness Russian spy. In fact, he probably was, and he was doing dirty business with the evil Jeffrey Getzstein. He had to be gathering intel on America's upper crust, juicy blackmail info with which the Russians could manipulate our wealthiest citizens and thus interfere with our politics and our democracy.

The nausea came back in waves. My legs felt weak. I needed a drink. One without gin or chocolate.

Gary propelled me from the room and out the sliding glass doors to the backyard. The stars were brilliant overhead, the flashing pool lights adding a kaleidoscope of psychedelic color. Nobody was swimming, the night air too cool for that, but the dance floor was packed, and the bars had long lines.

Fortunately, a pretty little server in a tux passed by with a tray of champagne. Gary thanked her, taking a large glass for each of us.

He clinked our glasses together. "Wish me luck, Coral. I'm about to take the biggest risk of my life."

I doubted that. But Rose was about to. And I planned to tell her exactly why she shouldn't.

Forcing a smile, I said, "Only the best for the best." Then I tossed back the bubbly like a pro.

Gary sipped his drink, nose in the air, pinky extended. He reeked of phony class. Get real, I thought as I searched the crowded yard for Rose. I had to save her, and fast.

The party was at a high pitch, the rap music way too loud, the dancing wild and overwrought. It looked like a rave for teenagers. How ridiculous...and potentially dangerous. Would these drunk children get behind the wheel of those expensive cars parked out front?

I spotted Doyle, talking to a thin woman with her

back to me. "I'll go ask Doyle where Rose is," I told Gary. "Stay put so she can find you." And so I can get to her first, I thought.

He nodded, complacent and, probably, worried sick that she'd fled due to a sudden case of cold feet.

One could always hope.

As I approached Doyle, he looked at me and said something to the woman. She glanced over her shoulder, and I recognized her with a start.

Getzstein's paramour.

I turned away, heading toward one of the bars, but it was too late. Doyle intercepted me before I could lose myself in the throng.

"Hey," he said. "Where've you been? I've been looking for you."

I gave him a hostile stare. "Where's Rose? Gary wants her."

More importantly, I needed to tell her why she should run as far as she could in the opposite direction.

"She left. Went home. She told me to tell you she thinks she caught your headache." He rolled those gorgeous green eyes of his, the innocent farm-boy eyes, the eyes of a man you could fall for and end up fatally wounded. "Whatever that means."

It was as if I had a mouthful of gasoline and his comment lit the fuse. I exploded. "It means she's tired of being lied to and shit on by asshole men."

His eyes widened then, and he sputtered. "I didn't mean—"

But I didn't want to hear what he had to say. It would be a lie, bullshit from yet another man unable to tell the truth. Even to those who loved him.

I slapped him across the face. Then I stormed off.

I headed for the side of the house, planning to leave the same way we'd come in. As I hurried down the path that curved through the trees, I noticed the door that led to the library. I stopped and stood there for a moment, thinking. Did I dare go back in for the evidence? Should I take the Russian passport with me? Proof, if Rose needed any to convince her not to run off with this man. This poser, this liar, this asshole who had stolen her heart. Twice!

A group of high school girls passed by, chatting and giggling. When I overheard one say *Jeffrey*, I began following them. I'd have to tell Rose what I knew without the hard evidence. It was too risky to take anything from him. He was a much bigger unknown than I'd imagined.

When I caught up to them, a freckled redhead with a tight ponytail was saying, "Yeah, and Giz says he pays two hundred for a massage. That's *so* much money."

A tall girl with long dark hair said, "I could use an infusion. Some of us don't have cushy towel girl jobs at Mar-a-Lago."

"Those jobs are just one step away from giving happy endings to rich dudes," a saucy looking blonde said.

The redhead fought back. "Your family buys you whatever you want. Mine can't. I need the cash to freaking *survive*."

The blonde shrugged. "We get it, Virginia. But you'd better be careful. You can fuck up your life getting involved with a man like that."

As we rounded the corner of the house and stepped into the front yard, I pushed past the girls. "You can fuck up your life getting involved with *any* man," I said.

The blonde laughed, but the other two just stared at me, their eyes large and guileless.

I hustled through the riotous crowd and headed down the pebbled drive. I wasn't watching where I was going because I was doing the math in my head. There were maybe ten million millionaires living in the US. If only one percent of the men were deviants, twists who wanted a go at a young girl—or boy—and each was willing to spend thousands of dollars for the opportunity to have sex with kids, well, someone was making a lot of money.

What if Getzstein was running a kind of playground, a brothel that offered underage girls? What if he shared the local teens with visitors to his estate and filmed these illegal interactions? He could charge the super wealthy pervs double—first for time with the children, then for repression of the evidence he'd collected on them.

When I got to the end of Gary's property, I scanned Doyle's driveway. Sure enough, Rose's Mercedes was gone. Hopefully, she had come to her senses. As I had come to mine. The situation was toxic, as was anyone associated with the not-so-great Getzstein.

I checked my watch. It wasn't all that late, so I decided to walk home. I really needed to calm down. My nerves were pinging, and electric jolts strummed my entire body. The nausea had settled down somewhat, but I still felt queasy. It wasn't all that far to Rose's, between three and four miles. The night was cool enough that I wouldn't sweat. And the moon would light my way.

I looked down at my nice flats, wishing I'd worn my running shoes. Oh well, I'd have blisters later, but I'd sleep well.

As I passed by Doyle's house with its sweet cottage charm, its romantic allure, I silently scolded myself for falling for a person lacking moral rectitude. What a disappointment he'd turned out to be. I was a reality instructor, but I couldn't tell Rose her cousin was laundering money for an infamous sex criminal. I would keep that ugly fact to myself, let her find out for herself what the boy was really made of. I would, however, inform her about Gary's passport. If she'd already decided not to run away with him, I wouldn't have to do any convincing. If not, and his secret Russian identity didn't change her mind, well, I'd have done my best.

I walked quickly, enjoying the night air. I wondered what had triggered Rose's swift escape, her decision to leave the party. All the little girls in tube tops and skinny jeans? The ominous presence of the local Madame? The frat house cheapness of the partygoers and the pointlessness of their drunken hilarity?

As I approached the Intracoastal bridge, I began to relax. My life didn't have to be here, in dirty Palm Beach. I could leave. I *should* leave. I would book a flight to Boston in the morning. The draft for my thesis was in much better shape. It was close to some kind of completion. It was time for me to return to reality. Time to leave the fantasy island behind. Again.

The bridge lights cast a muted orange glow against the moonlit sky, creating a mango backwash. As I climbed the gradual incline, the road beside me silent and faintly lit, I was hoping Virginia would change her mind about entering the soul-sucking world controlled by powerful male elites. The slope ahead might look like a gentle rise up a mountain of gold, but really, it was a fast slide down to hell.

At the peak of the incline, I stood by the cement guardrail overlooking the waterway. The moon was at the top of the sky now, a fat white face smiling down on us all. The encampment of homeless below me was still and quiet. Nobody was moving about, and the lapping water made a peaceful sound. In the distance, small fishing boats drifted, their green safety lights blinkering in the night.

When the moon slid behind a curtain of powder-puff clouds, I sighed.

Goodbye, moon. Goodbye, Palm Beach.

Epilogue
The End of a Once Poignant Story

The last thing I remember about that night is the eerie wail of tires skidding on asphalt, followed by a woman's piercing scream. Then, nothing.

When I woke up later, much later, my eyes were blurry, my mouth like sand. Doyle O'Henry was seated in a hot pink armchair beside the bed. He leaned toward me.

"Oh my god, you're okay." His eyes were full of tears.

I shut him down at once. I didn't know where I was or why, I had no idea what had happened to me. But I did recall very clearly what a shitbird he was.

"What are *you* doing here?" I said in a gravelly voice that did not sound like mine. I said some more things I can't recall. Exhausted, I closed my eyes again.

The next time I opened them, a strikingly handsome man in a starched white lab coat stood at my bedside. "Hullo," he said. "What have we here?"

I smiled up at him or tried to. My functions were slow, dysfunctional at best. Was I a total mess? Was my hair a nest of greasy tangles? I was pretty sure it was. When I reached up and touched it gingerly, he grinned.

"Looks like someone is feeling better."

"Someone would like to know where the hell she is. And what happened to her." I probed my arms and legs for casts and the like. Apparently, I was in the hospital. So what was wrong with me? "Am I okay?"

He nodded. "Yes, you are okay. You are a very lucky girl. Uh, woman. Person," he stumbled.

I laughed to myself. Serves men right. They don't even know how to address us anymore without getting shit for it.

Overcoming his discomfort, which was cute and quite appealing, he continued to explain in a stilted accent that I didn't recognize. "You were attacked and robbed on the east side of the Intracoastal bridge. They knocked you out, then fled. A local couple found you there, on the bridge, unconscious."

When I tried to sit up, my gorgeous doctor stepped in to help. He was delicious. Every good woman should be allowed to open her eyes one morning to a testosterone bonbon like him. Tall, dark, and super sexy, with a mane of thick black hair and an orthodontist's dream smile. My heart pitter-pattered. "So do I have any serious injuries?"

It didn't feel as though I did. Except for not recalling who'd mugged me, I felt okay. A bit stiff, maybe bruised about the ribs. I had a dreadful headache and a powerful thirst. But otherwise, not so bad. Better than on some hungover mornings.

My new crush said, "The head injury was only a concussion. But you must have needed the rest. You've been sleeping for two days now."

Was this a joke? They let me sleep here, in the hospital, with a concussion? I looked around. The room was fluffy and feminine, like a young girl's bedroom. Was I *not* in Palm Beach Memorial Hospital?

"Where *am* I?" I asked my hot doc.

"You're at Rose and Todd McCrary's home. They've put you up while you recover. We're in one of their second-floor bedrooms. The one they have decorated for their daughter to use when she is older." He pointed to a poster of that year's teenybopper heartthrob, Justin Bieber. "This is a little much, don't you think?"

I eased myself into a tenuous sitting position and reached over to the night table for what looked like a glass of water. He assisted, handing me a fat straw. Was he even a doctor? Doctors didn't hand you anything except bad news.

"Can you get Rose in here?" I asked him. "I'd like to speak to her."

He shook his head, black eyes downcast. "The McCrary family has gone on a 'round-the-world cruise. They don't expect to be back until next spring."

What?

I sucked at the warm water, which went down fast. What the hell? Had Todd kidnapped her? Or had they decided to run off together in order to escape the blowback from their affairs? Their sudden departure seemed so random, so impulsive.

Doctor Maybe refilled my empty glass from a silver pitcher of water. "They left me in charge of you. As soon as you feel well enough, you can go home. Okay?" he said, then he closed in on me, reached for me, his dark eyes bright with desire.

I shut my eyes, awaiting the medical prince's kiss.

He plumped up my pillow.

Okay, so he wasn't a doctor. A trained mental health aide maybe, but not a physician.

"Where's Doyle O'Henry?" I asked, avoiding his

sexy eyes as he continued to tend to me. He smoothed the sheets, but I kicked them off. I was in a nightgown, silky, pearl white, expensive. Probably one of Rose's.

"You sent him away, I'm afraid. Hasn't been back."

The memory of his presence in the chair beside the bed was foggy.

Sipping the water, I ran through everything recent I could recall. The party at Gary's, the library and his dark red Russian passport, the walk home, the bridge, and the bloated moon over the peaceful Intracoastal.

"I'd like to get dressed, if I may," I said, setting the water aside. I slid my legs carefully to one side of the small bed. "Are my clothes here?" I stood up with Not Doc's help.

"Mrs. McCrary said for you to borrow whatever you need. Your clothes had, well, blood on them. Wait here, I'll get you something from her closet."

I stopped him. "Take me with you. I need to walk around, get used to being on my feet again."

He took my arm, and we shuffled out of the room.

The situation was totally weird. Had someone drugged me? Why had I been unconscious for two days? And why had I been brought here, instead of to the local ER? Something smelled, and it wasn't Doctor No. As he helped me limp down the hall to the master bedroom, I thought he smelled like a clean rain. Very nice.

I was judging him by his cover, of course. And he'd passed the smell test, too.

By the time I stepped into Rose's closet, I was feeling almost normal. I grabbed clothes off a few hangers and dressed myself in a loose hippie skirt and a long spun-wool sweater. I was a vision of insanity in splotches of insistent pastels. I looked crazed, but I felt okay. Like I had freed myself of something. A weight, a burden. I wasn't sure what that was, but I was glad it was gone.

My caretaker hovered, but I dismissed his help. "Okay, so thank you for taking care of me. I guess I'll go back to the guest cottage and pack my stuff. Make a plane reservation."

He looked crestfallen. "Oh. Well, would you like to have dinner before you leave town?"

I thought about that. I was starving, apparently because I had gone for days without food. "Sure, as long as it's on the McCrarys' tab."

He walked me to my cottage and stood in the living room drinking coffee, which he brewed fresh, while I packed up all my stuff. My phone was missing. Obviously, it had been stolen during the robbery on the bridge. My laptop was missing, too, though, which I thought was very weird but didn't dare say anything about. I was starting to get suspicious of the whole situation.

A wave of paranoia swept over me. What if my gorgeous babysitter worked for the Russians? Maybe they wanted to know what *I* knew. About their plot to blackmail and manipulate the wealthy friends of Jeffrey Getzstein. About Gary Blass née Gavan Blazinskarov.

No matter. I knew nothing, really. Besides, I could get a new phone and laptop. And I'd saved the draft of my thesis to the cloud.

At my request, we went to The Horned Owl. Doctor Nobody drove us there in Rose's Mercedes. The afternoon sun rode low in the sky, the dry air a brisk—

for the tropics—sixty-eight degrees. Seasons do bring changes in South Florida, but the differences are subtle. Cold-loving plants bloom, deciduous trees drop leaves, and the sky boasts a stipple of high white clouds. Sometimes, the jet stream whisks far enough south to bring in a real cold spell, even a dusting of frost, but it never lasts long. Soon the sun beats down on your head again and you reach for your hat, your sunblock, and your designer shades. Most of the time you need to be a native to even notice the seasons.

The bar door was propped open, the interior unusually bright. I made my way carefully to the old oak bar while my companion parked the car. After I greeted Randy the barkeep, he served me a shot of bourbon from the bottom shelf.

Doctor In-the-Know seated himself beside me. I'd wanted to freak him out, drinking booze like that after a head injury, but he was totally chill.

"Make that two," he said, smiling at Randy.

Some medical professional he was turning out to be, letting me quaff hard liquor on top of a concussion, knockout drugs, and whatever else had been done to me.

"So, what's your name?" I asked after Randy served the man his drink.

"Business first," he responded with a wink. Or was that just the face he made whenever he drank run-of-the-mill bourbon? "I got you a first-class ticket to Boston. The plane leaves at ten tonight. I'd like to feed you a nutritious meal before you go. It has been a desire of mine since I was assigned to your case."

The bourbon tasted sweet and warming and cheap, yet very fine. "Are you a nutritionist?" I asked him, teasing.

He shrugged. "No, I am a concerned citizen. You haven't eaten, and you are recovering from a trauma. So grab a menu, and we will order you a good meal."

I was up for that, so I ordered a bunch of stuff from Randy. Tomato basil bisque, stuffed clams, salmon grilled with mushrooms and onions, a side of garlic spinach, and a double serving of French fries. My sponsor stuck with the booze, which I must admit I admired.

"So," I said, finishing my bourbon and signaling the bartender for another. My headache had disappeared, and I was clearheaded. Fresh. But a bit confused. "I need to know exactly what happened on the bridge."

He regarded me with an intense, inscrutable look on his handsome face. "You were attacked from behind, hit over the head with a blunt instrument, and robbed while unconscious. This was done to you by a homeless person or a group of them. The entire encampment along the waterway under the bridge has since been dispersed by the Palm Beach Police Department. The assailant or assailants were not identified, and your belongings were not recovered. A local citizen and his wife drove past after the incident and saw you lying on the sidewalk at the eastern end of the bridge, and they called 911."

The back of my head did not hurt. My headache had been interior. I felt around with one hand and found no bruises, no sore spots. I doubted I'd been hit on the skull. But all I said was, "Yeah, right. Blame it on the poor people."

His explanation sounded canned. Memorized like

the lines in a play. Rehearsed. Fake.

Randy brought over a shallow bowl of steaming soup, so I thanked him and dug in. Oh, it tasted good. I bent my head over the dish and spooned it in fast while my mind raced backward. I heard the screech of tires, my own scream. I'd been run down by a car, not mugged by a homeless person. Maybe a guest at Gary's party, a tipsy teen without a valid driver's license? Someone had sped across the bridge and veered over onto the sidewalk. I had no clear memory of the details, but I was damn sure I hadn't been beaten up.

Randy delivered more dishes. My date grinned at me, and I grunted like a pig in a poke. The spinach was hot, garlicky, yummy. I wolfed it down while reflecting on the private care I'd received, the days of unconsciousness, and the feeling of having been drugged. Obviously, I'd been hidden away from the press, from any kind of investigation.

When I finished the greens, I reached for the fries. Why was I being rushed out of town? Why no police interview about the crime that had been committed against me? My situation was obviously not an everyday robbery. No, it was another Palm Beach cover-up. Somebody had paid somebody else to spare them the public embarrassment. Or the exposure.

"This is bullshit," I said between bites of crispy, greasy potato. "I mean, on what evidence was the assumption made that the encampment was responsible? And how did I end up in the Justin Bieber room at Rose's instead of the ER at PBMH?"

He shrugged. "I came on the case after you became a private nursing patient. So I can't answer that."

He was a nurse? He didn't look like a nurse. And

he'd booked my flight home. What kind of nurse serves as a travel agent too?

The lying kind.

"So who do you work for?" I asked him, diving into the salmon. Pink with a crispy crust, it was juicy, mushroomy, oniony, delicious.

He stared at me, his dark eyes like wells. Black holes a girl could fall into and keep on falling. "I work for Jeffrey Getzstein. Everyone in this town works for the great Getzstein." He tipped his almost empty glass at me. "In some way or another."

Then he finished his bourbon and ordered another.

Later, I had a big wedge of hot apple pie with a melting scoop of French vanilla ice cream. For an unassuming bar, The Horned Owl served up superb comfort food.

****

Years went by before they caught up with some of the players. You probably know most of the story. Everyone knows what happened to Jeffrey Getzstein. The national news covered the salacious details on his arrest for solicitation, the light sentence he was given in a cushy Palm Beach jail, followed by the long undercover investigation and threat of real prison time, and culminating in his very public arrest and shocking jailhouse suicide.

Only the best for the best.

Gary had remained in Palm Beach, possibly hoping for the return of his true love. He no longer hosted parties and rarely went out of the house, which slid into a striking state of disrepair. The island gossip was vicious. Nothing like the downfall of new money to get old money's tongues wagging and slashing. Lead rumor was that Gary had worked for Getzstein, gathering intel on high-profile Americans and their kids who overindulged themselves at his parties. Hidden cameras in every bedroom and bathroom—surveillance capitalism at its very best.

Had he seen footage of me looking at his passport? Of course. Had he thought I still had it and jumped in his car to run me down on the bridge? Possibly. Someone had, and they'd gotten away with it.

In the fall of 2008, Gary "Blass" Blazinskarov was found floating facedown in his pool, dead from an overdose of opioids. His suicide was never investigated. I have my suspicions about that. Todd had friends who had friends, if you know what I mean. Then again, Gary knew a lot of people who knew other people. There were indications he was underwater with nowhere to go but down. Like so many people around that time, Gary was in way over his head financially, and the cement anklets of foreclosure clutched tight at his feet.

And then there were the Russians. Also his work with Getzstein. Gary wasn't popular anymore. He had a lot of reasons to die.

Doyle returned to North Dakota and married the apple-cheeked Lauren. I saw the wedding photos on her Facebook page. She looked thrilled—and about eight months pregnant. I hoped she didn't mind having a husband with a moral compass pointing south. His cover is respectable but highly misleading.

Rose and Todd went back to living like royalty in Palm Beach, this time in a different castle, an even bigger one, even more ostentatious. Or so I heard. I haven't seen it. Haven't been invited. My bestie stopped communicating with me after my "accident." I figure this is either because she did not want to be reminded about her affair with a man who lacked real status, or because she knew her lover ran me down on the bridge. I love her, but our friendship was of another time. Just like her affair with Gary Blass.

I've kept my distance from all of them. Safer that way. I stopped snooping, too. I preferred to live. But of this I am sure. Somebody with money or connections or both hit me on that bridge, then paid their way out of criminal charges for driving under the influence and leaving the scene of an accident. Or attempted homicide. Take your pick, but that's how it goes in *über*-wealthy enclaves like Palm Beach.

I was sorry to hear how Jeffrey Getzstein went down for the count. I'd rather have seen him admit his guilt in court and pay amends to those he hurt, but at least he lost all status. Did he really commit suicide in his jail cell, or was he murdered? If he'd talked, the cushy private lives of a lot of very important people would've been threatened. The same can be said for Gary.

Nowadays, nobody in Palm Beach admits to having known the great Getzstein. They all act like he never lived in their midst, tempting the young girls with cash, the wealthy men with underage sex. But the world knows the story of the rich bachelor who supplied teens to old politicians, businessmen, and royalty. The world knows and is scandalized, titillated, and rapt.

With the Great Recession, the posers left the island in humiliated droves. Some took up residence in local tent cities. Others hitched a ride north to do honest or not-so-honest work.

My own life was a struggle for a while. I taught

environmental biology to homeschool students while finishing my thesis. My aunt passed away, finally. But to everyone's surprise, the old lady was nearly broke. I inherited a large library of her autographed books and a substantial mortgage.

Still, I wanted to move back home. Boston was cold and gray, and I missed the Florida sunsets, the starry night sky, the bleak cry of the herons. I missed the white sand beaches, the pounding surf, the wild and sudden bursts of cool rain. I missed the coral reefs, which would one day be gone.

So I moved to my aunt's house, published my thesis as a literary ecology book, and got an adjunct position at the local community college. I started seeing sexy Doctor No, but he's too dodgy for me.

They say South Florida is a sunny place for shady characters, and it's true. I'm trying hard not to become one of them. It's a life goal that I reach for like a flashing light in the distance. An ideal life, one I can almost grasp.

Addendum
Excerpts from
Coral on Coral

Sea rocks, salt wind scrapes
the silver musical waves
the skin from your upturned face
which wears the weather
like a flag, a tan tattoo
of the harsh parts of Florida.

There's an aura of tarnished
brass, menace and hurt.
Inside your sunken chest
the heart box has emptied
out and the tin rhythm
echoes, fleeing
with the easterly breeze.

You have soul trouble,
the depths before you
destroyed by such humanity.

You look to the horizon,
a mango crush under blue,
for answers, for a future
knowing there's nothing
but what you've already made.

Below you the ocean spits up green
from a deep lung infection that sickens
all life as we know it—that
enough answer for you?

Watch the ancient reef
crumbling below
bleaching away
struggling to sustain
all hues except sad gray
all life fails to thrive
like babies starved to the bone.

Exoskeletons toss and turn
like ash on the tide.

****

White gulls hover
drafting on a dark wind
their adulterous eyes,
strange wild cries.
Shorebirds bicker
over tiny wriggles of fish
peppered across wet sand.
A lone blue heron
stick legged, aristocratic
standing guard, long bill
pointed east. Royal
terns mob a friend
hoarding small catch,
irate juveniles
squawk for a share.

Between your toes, rippled
seaweed plaits and today's find—
half-hearted stone
glass balls, sea smudged
cobalt blue with aqua spray
like miniature globes.
There's puka like baby teeth
Portuguese man o' war washed up,
an army of the dead.
You collect coral chunks
in melon and cream, once
more alive
with a more important role
in this life
than you ever had.

The rain pelts down
pinging the restless sea
drowning the plastic gifts
that slosh up the tideline
leaving brightly colored coin
with infinite negative value
scattered across the world
choking, poisoning—ruination.

You want to save everything
bring it all home with you
in a safe deposit box.

Torn between running away
and going in deeper
you wait eons too long
before the ocean spreads

its undulant magic carpet
like an unfurling tongue
to lap you up

and you step off the beach
and into the warm hand of the sea
for one more ride.

****

The coral kisses your bare skin
where the flippers begin, eyes
wide behind a dewy mask
as you kick your way past
fanning trees and ragged cliffs
softened by a salted fog,
wild crag sculptures
the pink of baby's cheeks
burnt umber, rose, tangerine, green
and coral, sweet peach
colors that burst through
the dream you are in
an underwater fantasyland.

Nature's richest garden
that has, scientists say,
thirty years left to live—
or less.

And here you are
killing it
with carbon
we emit so mindlessly
our cars and farms

planes and heated homes
new this, new that
the joyride of our lives.

Don't look now
but we're coming to a hard boil
and below us
mass bleaching events
mass underwater destruction
of our ocean rainforests
across less than one percent
of the mysterious sea floor
more than a million species
including one-quarter of all fish
in the coral forests they call home.

We kill them
in their own homes.

If we want to be more selfish
we can acknowledge how
the reefs protect us
from storms and sea rise,
surges and hurricanes,
erosion that takes away travel
vacations and waterfront mansions
and the wealth of the land
we claim for ourselves
alone.

****

Beyond the city's glare
the surface of black water

lies still, rippling, neon
lipstick red, bleach blonde
veiny blue, bruised purple
colors that move
and blur, smearing
reflections of tall buildings
ornate mansions, condos, new
developments afloat
built to not last, built up
and gnawing on the shore.

Rash water closes in
sea grass breathing
the warm night air
that whispers of bad things
to come.

The wind rests sometimes
the smell lingering, pungent
as unwashed feet,
twisted fish bones
dead brain matter
seaflesh gone bad.

This is a moment of dangerous, lustrous splendor
and you
with a smile like
a homemade explosive device—
you want only the best
for the best and
the next move
is all
yours.

About the Author

Mickey J. Corrigan lives in South Florida, where the men run guns and the women run after them. She writes crazy romance and sexy psychological thrillers. Her stories have been called "delightful pulp," "oh so compulsive" reads, and "bizarre but believable." Books include the mad love series The Hard Stuff and the two darkly romantic comedies *The Blow Off* and *Ex-Treme Measures*, all from The Wild Rose Press, Inc. Most recently, she's published quirky crime novels with small literary presses in the UK, *Project XX* from Salt and *What I Did for Love* from Bloodhound Books.

~*~

Visit Mickey at
http://www.mickeyjcorrigan.com